CHRISTINA LAUREN

Beautiful BELOVED

GALLERY BOOKS
NEW YORK   AMSTERDAM/ANTWERP   LONDON
TORONTO   SYDNEY/MELBOURNE   NEW DELHI

G

Gallery Books
An Imprint of Simon & Schuster, LLC
1230 Avenue of the Americas
New York, NY 10020

For more than 100 years, Simon & Schuster has championed authors and the stories they create. By respecting the copyright of an author's intellectual property, you enable Simon & Schuster and the author to continue publishing exceptional books for years to come. We thank you for supporting the author's copyright by purchasing an authorized edition of this book.

No amount of this book may be reproduced or stored in any format, nor may it be uploaded to any website, database, language-learning model, or other repository, retrieval, or artificial intelligence system without express permission. All rights reserved. Inquiries may be directed to Simon & Schuster, 1230 Avenue of the Americas, New York, NY 10020 or permissions@simonandschuster.com.

This book is a work of fiction. Any references to historical events, real people, or real places are used fictitiously. Other names, characters, places, and events are products of the author's imagination, and any resemblance to actual events or places or persons, living or dead, is entirely coincidental.

Copyright © 2015 by Christina Hobbs and Lauren Billings

All rights reserved, including the right to reproduce this book or portions thereof in any form whatsoever. For information, address Gallery Books Subsidiary Rights Department, 1230 Avenue of the Americas, New York, NY 10020.

First Gallery Books trade paperback edition July 2025

GALLERY BOOKS and colophon are registered trademarks of Simon & Schuster, LLC

Simon & Schuster strongly believes in freedom of expression and stands against censorship in all its forms. For more information, visit BooksBelong.com.

For information about special discounts for bulk purchases, please contact Simon & Schuster Special Sales at 1-866-506-1949 or business@simonandschuster.com.

The Simon & Schuster Speakers Bureau can bring authors to your live event. For more information or to book an event, contact the Simon & Schuster Speakers Bureau at 1-866-248-3049 or visit our website at www.simonspeakers.com.

Manufactured in the United States of America

10 9 8 7 6 5 4 3 2 1

Library of Congress Cataloging-in-Publication Data has been applied for.

ISBN 978-1-6680-7839-6
ISBN 978-1-4767-9165-4 (ebook)

PRAISE FOR CHRISTINA LAUREN

"You can never go wrong with a Christina Lauren novel."
—*Entertainment Weekly*

"Christina Lauren's books are . . . the gold standard for romance novels."
—*BuzzFeed*

"There's nothing more fun than Christina Lauren."
—Katherine Center,
New York Times bestselling author

"I absolutely devoured this book . . . some of the most delicious spice I have read in a long time."
—JoAnna Garcia Swisher,
actress and founder of The Happy Place,
on *The Paradise Problem*

"My favorite kind of book to devour: something that manages to be hot and intense, yet still the very best comfort food."
—Jodi Picoult,
#1 *New York Times* bestselling author,
on *The True Love Experiment*

"Required beach reading."
—*Oprah Daily* on *Something Wilder*

"Sweet and steamy!"
—*USA Today* on *In a Holidaze*

BOOKS BY CHRISTINA LAUREN

Dating You / Hating You
Roomies
Love and Other Words
Autoboyography
Josh and Hazel's Guide to Not Dating
My Favorite Half-Night Stand
The Unhoneymooners
Twice in a Blue Moon
The Honey-Don't List
In a Holidaze
The Soulmate Equation
Something Wilder
The True Love Experiment
*Honeymoon Crashers**
The Paradise Problem
Tangled Up in You

THE BEAUTIFUL SERIES

Beautiful Bastard
Beautiful Stranger
Beautiful Bitch
Beautiful Bombshell
Beautiful Player
Beautiful Beginning
Beautiful Beloved
Beautiful Secret
Beautiful Boss
Beautiful

THE WILD SEASONS SERIES

Sweet Filthy Boy
Dirty Rowdy Thing
Dark Wild Night
Wicked Sexy Liar

YOUNG ADULT

The House
Sublime

*Audiobook only

For our readers.
Thank you for missing Max and Sara,
and wanting more.

Hello, Beautifuls!

Look at this, all of us together—still—after eleven glorious years!

It's hard to believe that much time has passed . . . but then we think about all the smiling faces we've met on tours, the hugs you've given us, the artwork you've created, the books you've proudly written and shared with us, and it starts to feel like a lifetime ago that these books came out.

Going back through these—for the sake of nostalgia and editing, of course—is a trip. It's tempting to want to update things here and there, from little details like locations that no longer exist to more important things like making consent clearer in *Beautiful Bastard*. But our editor and friends gently reminded us that these books are the first we ever wrote; we need to cherish that raw newness, from the clear exuberance we wrote with to the texts' occasional dated flaws. We are starkly reminded of the adage *books can't change, but writers can*.

So, we step back and look at the *Beautiful* series from a greater distance, gained from both time and experience, and what we see is something truly magical: a series that launched a partnership dozens of books deep, that gave us a readership that provides us with so much energy and inspiration, that created this career for us we are grateful for every day. We are so thrilled that we get to give it new life with this repackage and re-release.

And we hope you love the new look and the familiar words inside. Thank you for being with us all this time, or if you've just discovered us, please join us in laughing about traitor nipples and the man who hides ripped underwear in his desk. No matter what, we both hope you all have fun digging (back) into these. It's been the wildest, most spectacular ride of our lives.

With massive affection,

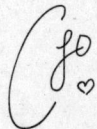

One

MAX

The dishes were done, the flat tidied, and Sara had begun to sing quietly to our little miss in the nursery. I said a simple prayer to the god of sleeping children, because on her way in there, Sara had given me the look.

The *don't fall asleep before I come to bed* look.

The *I'm still not over the sight of our baby sleeping on your naked chest* look.

The *you're getting very, extremely laid* look.

I fucking loved my life.

Across the room on the coffee table, my phone lit up with a call. Going over and seeing whose name flashed across the screen, I broke out in a massive smile.

"You've called the happiest bloke on the planet," I told my brother, in lieu of a proper greeting.

I was met with a heavy pause of silence, and then: "It's impossible for you to be smugger."

"True. But make it quick. I'm about to be ravaged by the natives." Sweet mother Mary it seemed like it'd been forever since we'd had anything more than a quick grope en route to passing out from exhaustion.

I was even considering doing some extensive stretching first.

My youngest brother, Niall, laughed. "In that case, I hope you survive the night because I'm coming to visit next week and I'd be terribly disappointed to miss the Max Stella tour you've promised all these years."

"Brilliant!" I smacked the table with my palm. This night kept getting better. The promise of sex two nights in a row with my gorgeous wife and a visit from my brother next week. "Absolutely, bloody brilliant." I hadn't seen Niall since the last time I went home, over a year ago, and he'd been too busy to visit much. "Work letting you out, then?"

"More or less." He paused. "Right. That's it, then, it's bloodly late. Just letting you know. I'm coming to visit little Annabel, not you lot."

Laughing, I said, "Understood."

"I'll arrive on Tuesday. Leaving Sunday."

I noted the rest of the details and rang off before heading to find Sara to share the news.

The singing had stopped, and to my complete lack of surprise, I found my beautiful wife asleep in the rocking chair, with the baby in her arms. I pulled the little Beloved away from her mum and placed her in the crib. Although until recently Annabel generally slept only two or three hours at a time, at least we could put her to bed beside a brass band and she wouldn't rouse.

I suspected we wouldn't be as lucky with the next one. *Next one?*

I blinked, feeling slightly mad for having this thought. It was only in the past two weeks that we were getting any sort of decent sleep at all.

With the baby taken care of, I woke Sara. Her eyes drew open just as I reached her, and she inhaled deeply, blinking up at me. "Oh. I fell asleep."

I crouched in front of her, using my thumb to move a strand of hair off her face. "I don't think you were supposed to do that."

"No, I was going to get you naked."

"That's still an option."

Sara took my hand and stood, pulling me after her out of the nursery and down the hall. "What were you thinking, just standing there looking down at me?"

"Just feeling rather in love with my life, is all."

"Well, I fell asleep wondering whether our second will be as good a sleeper as our first."

She glanced over her shoulder at me with a grin, and I gaped at her, eyes wide and incredulous. How could she know the exact thought had crossed my mind only minutes before?

"You call Anna a *good sleeper*?" I asked.

"She has been lately," she clarified. "We just had to give her time to grow into it."

I watched Sara's hair slide over her shoulders as she turned back and shook her head. Her hair was longer now, thicker, and the way it slid across her skin made me want to gather it into a ball, hold it in my fist, and fuck her over the side of the bed.

Oh, but it had been forever since we'd done anything as rough as that.

I swallowed, closed my eyes, and attempted to steady my hunger when she sat on the edge of the mattress and slowly slid her thighs apart.

"You've lost your mind," I said with a grin.

"Probably true." Her sexy little shrug told me she was only half serious, and a naughty playfulness lingered beneath the surface.

Stepping between her legs, I helped her pull her tank top over her head and guided her onto her back so I could slide her thin cotton shorts down and off.

Slow, Max.

My mind frenzied with thoughts of pushing her thighs to her chest, biting my way down her torso, sucking and spanking the sweetness between her legs until she screamed so loud it shook the walls. Instead, I kissed her navel, her hip, moving my mouth to her ribs and then up higher to the firm swell of her breasts. They were already full, and growing tight the longer the baby slept. I bent, sucking at the pink flush of her nipples.

"Do you really love to look at them so much?" Her voice dropped slightly. "You like the taste?"

I *loved* her body like this, but I didn't know how to truly admit it. I loved her hips, her breasts. Loved to watch her feed our baby and come curl around me after. It felt like every fucking thing in the world had come together with the arrival of our daughter. But it still felt a bit shameful to want her body to stay this way after what had admittedly been a tough labor.

I shifted forward carefully, pressing my cock through my boxers into the warm skin between her legs.

Sara pulled me down over her and slid her mouth down my neck. "Is it weird that I want to stay like this?" she asked as I spread my hand over her hip. "To fill this home of ours with little ankle biters?"

I laughed into her shoulder. "Sleep deprivation is eating your brain."

"I know you want a big family," she said. "And I've never been more in love with you than when I've seen you be a daddy . . ." She noticed where my attention had gone, to the firm swell of her breast again, my mouth closing over her nipple. "They get full like this . . ."

I kissed my way up to her neck. "They provide me with a rather spiritual experience."

"So you *do* like my body right now?" she whispered.

There was a delicate edge to her voice, a vulnerability that shocked me. Sara knew I loved her body, every inch of her perfect, soft skin.

Didn't she?

I pulled back to look at her. "I fucking *love* your body. And I love how happy motherhood has made you. I like how you seem rather blissful lately." Bending, I spoke into the warm space between her breasts: "I also like how ripe your tits are."

She took a handful of my hair and pulled me back, laughing. "Finally, he admits it!"

"What does that mean?"

Her brow furrowed a little as she studied my face, warm brown eyes moving to take in every aspect of my expression. Sara often studied me like this: quietly, earnestly. She ran a fingertip across my chin, her eyes trained on my lips. "I want you to not worry so much," she whispered. "I want more babies—maybe not right away, but someday—and when I say that, I see terror in your eyes."

I swallowed around the heavy lump in my throat. "It's not as hard on my body."

"My body seems to be weathering it fine. I'm going back to work soon. Look at us. We *did* it."

I bent, tasting her skin again. Kissing her stomach.

She pulled me up, whispered in my ear, "Tell me you didn't love having your baby in here."

Laughing, I admitted, "She was certainly easier to take care of all tucked away in there."

She looked back up at my face as I shifted over her, spreading her thighs with my knee and settling there, growing tighter at the feel of her, soft and warm, beneath me. "All right, love?"

Her breaths were already coming faster, short bursts against my neck, her hands sliding lower over my back to push my boxers down my hips. "Yeah."

I slipped my finger into her mouth, wetting it against her tongue before bringing it between us to touch her. I hummed, rubbing myself on her thigh. "You sure? You're not sore?"

She stared up at me, expression shifting into one I couldn't quite read. "I'm *sure*."

"We made love last night, too. I don't want to hurt you," I explained.

She closed her eyes, pulling my head into her neck. "I know, baby."

I slid in, slow, and pressed my mouth to her jaw, groaning. Each time . . . each fucking time I was sure I would never get used to the feel of her. Her nails dug into my back as she let out a relieved moan.

"Christ, Petal. You're heaven beneath me." Cupping her breast in one hand, I squeezed, relishing the slide of milk on my palm. "Fuck," I managed. "*Fucking hell . . .*"

"This is a new thing," she whispered, scratching her nails down my back.

I clenched my jaw, fighting the admission that wanted to burst free. "I bloody love them like this. I'm sorry—I know they're mostly a drag for you—but fuck, Petal. I love your tits like this."

I felt her still beneath me and stopped moving so I could pull back and look at her face.

"What?" I asked. "What did I say?"

She didn't look upset, just a funny mix of disappointed and amused. Sliding her legs up my sides, she whispered, "Since when do you have to give me a disclaimer?"

Smiling, I bent and kissed her sweet, full lips. My heart was beating a little too fast; I still wasn't sure what I'd done wrong.

"You don't have to apologize for being turned on by that," she whispered into my mouth. "I miss seeing you lost in me, and unapologetic about it."

My immediate instinct was to *show* her how lost I really was: to lift her arms over her head, pound into her, and relish the sight of her breasts moving below me, relish their weight and the spike of lust I felt when they leaked onto my skin. But instead, I began to slowly move above her, making sure to ease her pleasure from her with every draw of my body inside hers.

She grabbed my ass, urged me faster and harder, and

I tried to give her more but it was almost like something newly hardwired in me with every shift forward:

Take it easy.
Take it slow.
Take it easy.
Take it slow.

We'd had sex many times in the months since the baby was born, but it hadn't yet returned to the wild days of before, with fucking on the kitchen table or the floor, or sweaty and reckless play in the club. Those days we'd had spanking and bondage. Those days I'd taken her in every manner imaginable, sometimes with strangers watching, sometimes with only my video camera as witness. Once I'd bit her shoulder so hard she'd bled and it nearly made her savage with excitement.

Before—and during—her pregnancy, it never occurred to me how *fragile* she was.

And then she'd had my baby: nearly nine pounds and over twenty-four hours of hard labor. For two months after Annabel came, we'd stumbled our way through new parenting, fallen in love with our daughter, fallen in love all over again with each other, and found tiny winks of sleep whenever we could. Eventually, we'd also found ways to be carefully intimate with hands and mouths, playful with words and toys.

Then, nearly two months ago now, Sara said she was ready to make love again.

I'd been terrified at first, but one kiss led to another, and soon I'd been harder than I could remember being in weeks. The sound she made when I pushed into her would forever echo in my thoughts. It was a broken sound, the sharp, surprised cry of pain. I'd immediately stopped, and although she swore she felt no pain *now*, I couldn't help but feel I was handling her differently: being careful with a treasure I'd only recently discovered could be broken . . .

We had yet to return to the club.

We had yet to even pull out the camera for anything other than pictures of our daughter.

We had yet to have sex that did anything more than rustle the sheets, let alone break furniture.

But here, in our bed, with her beneath me, and making her hungry, gasping little noises, her words echoed in my head—*pounding*—each one like a mallet hitting a drum.

I miss seeing you lost in me, and unapologetic about it.

She was letting me be gentle. She was patiently waiting for it to sink in that she'd asked for more, for real sex, again and again.

She'd say, *Do you want to make a movie tonight?*

No, Petal, it's enough just to feel you.

Do you ever miss the club?

No, Petal, I love being right here where we are, with our baby asleep down the hall.

You really like to look at them like this? You like the taste?

I'd wanted to make things easy for her. I'd wanted her

to feel safe and cherished. I closed my eyes, absorbed by the paradoxical sensations of relief when Sara began to quietly come beneath me, and heartache in the realization that somewhere along the line, I had forgotten what she needed.

༄

AT FOUR IN THE morning, I sat on the floor of the nursery while Sara fed Annabel. The sky outside was deep blue-black, and even on the Upper East Side at this hour, the streets were relatively quiet.

"You didn't have to get up with us," she whispered.

She said the same thing every morning, worried about my lack of sleep and a long workday ahead. But this, right here, was my favorite part of the day.

"I'll bundle her up and go for a run when you're done."

Sara watched me in the darkness. "I love you."

I swallowed, nodding as I struggled to work past the lump in my throat so I could repeat the sentiment. I'd barely been able to sleep last night after realizing I'd been so focused on enjoying Sara the Mother that I'd barely let myself enjoy Sara the Woman.

"What's wrong?" she whispered, watching me struggle.

"I think we need to make a deal to return to us before we can get pregnant again."

"'Us'?" she repeated.

"I think I heard what you were saying last night."

Her brows pulled together and I could tell she wasn't exactly sure what I was saying. "Oh?"

"I want to be the husband you need again. Photographs. Film. Knowing I'm giving you what you need."

"What I need?"

"What *we* need."

She licked her lips, blinking down to the baby. "You're so much more than I could have ever hoped for. You know that."

"I'd like to occasionally outdo myself," I said, and she giggled, putting her hand over her mouth when the baby pulled off her breast in surprise.

"Shh, shh," Sara murmured to her. "Come here."

"Maybe Mum can watch little Beloved and we can start with dinner out? Slowly work our way to something else?"

She looked up again, eyes wide. "Like the club?"

I watched her holding our child in her arms and felt a protectiveness so violent lash over me I wasn't sure how I would handle letting others see her so vulnerable, so *ripe*.

"If that's what you want," I managed.

She nodded, gently answering the question in my voice. "It is."

∽

I FOLDED UP THE stroller and stowed it in the foyer closet before stripping off my shirt. Although so far it had been a mild winter, it was still January and the long-sleeved running shirt I wore to keep me from freezing outside immediately felt claustrophobic upon entering the warm apartment.

Bending, I unzipped the carrier and pulled out the extremely bundled child inside.

"Was that good, baby girl?" I murmured, kissing her pink cheek. She was warm and drooly and her enormous brown eyes crinkled exactly like her mother's when she smiled. "Got a good run in, didn't we?"

I sat on the couch and laid Annabel on my chest while I caught my breath.

"You're sweaty and sitting on the couch, aren't you?" Sara called from the master suite.

I stuck my tongue out at Anna and she tried to grab it. "Very sweaty," I answered my wife. "Quite disgusting, actually."

Sara's heels clicked down the hallway and she froze when she saw us. "Max."

"I'll wipe it down, Pet—"

"I don't care about that," she said, walking closer. "You're shirtless with the world's sweetest baby cuddled on those muscles. Put a shirt on, you beast, or I can't be held responsible for my actions."

I fucking loved it when Sara looked at me like that. "Imagine how I feel when you're feeding her."

She gave me a bright smile as she bent, kissing Anna's chubby thigh. "She looks like a little peach on you."

I took in her outfit and immediately wondered if we'd be able to get the baby down for a nap this early in the day. I hadn't seen Sara in work clothes in months and didn't realize until just then how much I missed it. Her little black skirt hit just below her knees, giving a tiny flash of skin above her soft leather boots. Her tits looked fucking unreal in the gray sweater she'd put on.

Following my attention, she looked down at her chest. "I think I need to go shopping today. Everything is too small in the chest."

"Don't you dare get rid of that one."

She pulled her lip between her teeth, blinking over to me. "Yeah?"

"Yeah," I murmured, and the moment grew heavy. "You look bloody beautiful, Petal."

"Is it . . . inappropriate, though? I mean, the way you're looking at me makes me think this sweater is no longer very professional."

"I guess it depends on where you're headed."

She shrugged, sitting down next to us. "I thought I'd go into the office for a couple of hours, just so next week doesn't feel so disorienting. I'm meeting the girls for breakfast and then heading in."

I kissed the top of Anna's head. "Want me to take her with me?"

"Either way. I could, too."

What was it about her face in that moment, right there, that made me feel so many things at once it was overwhelming? With her dressed and headed out the door, it was like I was seeing this combination for the first time: my lover, my wife, and also a mother, a nurturer and . . . *fuck*, a bird with the best pair of tits I'd ever seen.

Standing, I motioned for her to follow me back down the hall. I grabbed Annabel's musical baby seat from the nursery and put it beside the dresser in our bedroom, facing the set of framed photographs of trees that she loved, and then guided Sara to the bed.

"*Max* . . ."

"Just a minute." I retrieved my camera from the shelf, stabilized it on the tripod, and set it to automatic shots every five seconds. Sara's breath was rapid and shallow when I bent low, kissed her neck, and told her, "I won't keep you long."

"Anna's fine," she said, pulling me closer. "Keep me as long as you can."

Laying her back, I pushed her skirt up her hips and began kissing my way up her stomach, feeling my cock tighten with each nostalgic click of the shutter, with the feel of her hands digging into my hair. I moved her sweater up her stomach, revealing smooth, bare skin. She tasted like rain, like fruit, and had the same sweet scent I'd always worshipped on her body. Reaching behind her, I unhooked her bra and pushed it up over her breasts.

I'd always loved Sara's breasts but I'd never particularly been a breast man until recently. The weight of them, the soft smell of her skin, and the odd spike I felt in my abdomen whenever she fed our child . . . it was an odd reflex to want to look at them, touch them like this, and one I realized I'd been fighting the last few months.

You don't have to apologize for being turned on by that.

My mouth closed over the peak, tongue pulling her deeper into my mouth, and I groaned at the feel of it. She was warm and firm, so full—

I did this . . .

I made her this way

—and when she reached for my track pants and pushed them down my hips to take me in her hand, the moment dissolved into frenzy.

I could imagine her looking through the pictures later, seeing how much I relished the feel of her in my mouth, the taste of her on my tongue. She would know, then, just by looking at my face, how I loved the slide of milk on my hand, the way her hips looked spread around mine. I worshipped her.

I bloody worshipped this woman.

I rocked into her fist, groaning at the feel of her mouth sucking at my neck, her desperate, sweet little cries into my skin. Shoving her panties aside, I licked my hand and used it to make her slick so I could push deep inside with one sharp stab of my hips.

She gasped, eyes wide with thrill and relieved—fuck, she was *relieved*, as if I'd been missing and maybe I had. I pulled out and shifted forward, fucking her so hard and fast that within the span of a minute I knew I was coming; coming before I had time to get her there, before I even had time to consider whether she wanted me to spill inside her before leaving for work. I just . . . *wanted* with such intensity, with a kind of jagged need I hadn't felt in so long that I couldn't seem to slow myself down.

The tenderness and protectiveness had been pushed aside, just for the moment, by something older and familiar: a heavy need to claim her.

I reached between us, playing with her with my fingertips until she was bucking into my hand, gasping and squeezing around my cock. She cried out, three sharp pleas to drag her through her pleasure, and then she fell quiet, pulling me fully on top of her and exhaling heavily into my neck.

She'd seen me every day; we'd cuddled, talked, laughed, fallen asleep at the dinner table together, and done all manner of intimate things. But the relief in this moment was profound. I knew exactly what she meant when she whispered, "I missed you."

And all I could say back was "I missed you, too."

Mum was already at her desk when I arrived at the office wearing Annabel in the carrier. She jumped up, ran around the desk, and reached for her granddaughter without even looking at my face.

"Mum," I hissed, laughing as I reached for her shoulders so she wouldn't jostle the baby. "She's asleep. Settle down, woman. You'll get her in a bit when I've got a meeting with Levinson."

My mother looked up at me and replaced her mild scowl with a sweet smile. "Mornin', love."

I'd never seen myself as a mum's boy growing up but having her with us at Stella & Sumner for the past several years was one of my favorite things about coming to work. Especially since we'd had Annabel, I appreciated the proximity of family and their ability to tell us when we were acting like neurotic idiots.

And although Mum had raised ten of us quite capably, I registered I was due for a sizable heap of shit when I asked her—for the first time—to watch the baby so we could go out. We'd always taken the baby with us, but this was . . . well, this was entirely different.

"Mum," I started as she walked back around her desk to sit down. "I was hoping to take Sara out this coming Friday. Would you mind heading over and watching Annabel?"

Her face fell. "Max, you forgot."

I groaned. *Fuck.* This was the second time a woman had said this to me in less than twenty-four hours. "Forgot what?"

"I leave for Leeds tomorrow, dove. I'm going to stay with Karen for three weeks."

"Aw, bugger."

"I can watch her tonight?"

"No, you've got to pack and we don't have any sort of plan in place. I get the sense we'll both need this to be a military operation."

"You're mental. I've been telling you for weeks: just take the wife out and have some dinner, for crying out loud. By the time you and Niall and Rebecca came along, we were letting the dog watch you for a night out."

Laughing, I agreed, "I don't doubt it."

꩜

"THE FUCK ARE YOU wearing?"

I looked down at Annabel still asleep in the carrier and replied to Will, "It's called an Ergo."

He followed me into my office and sat on my couch. "It looks like you went tandem skydiving and forgot to unlatch."

Bennett walked up behind him. "You look like a marsupial."

"It's called baby wearing, you twats." I laughed, and

then whispered to the baby, "Is that right? Are you my little joey?" I looked up at my mates and only then did I do the mental calculation. "Bennett, what the hell are you doing here?"

"Will and I had a meeting with Gross and Barrett at eight. Did you forget?"

"Bloody hell will you lot cut me some slack! I've not slept in four fucking months!"

They both stared at me, wide-eyed, for several silent seconds.

"Are your nipples sore?" Will asked.

I shook my head, laughing. "Tosser."

As carefully as I could, I unhooked the carrier behind my neck and let it fall so I could lay Anna down on the couch beside Will. She startled—both arms and both legs flying out in a spasm—but then immediately fell back asleep.

For his part, Will looked like I'd just put a giant hollow eggshell near him. His hands were clasped in his lap and his eyes were trained on the baby as if she might suddenly roll and explode. He'd been around Anna nearly every weekend since she'd been born and still looked at her like breathing too heavily near her might cause her to shatter.

"Since when are you an idiot around children?" I asked.

"I love kids," he said, looking up at me. "But she's just so *little*."

"She's not," I assured him. "She's enormous."

"You know what I mean."

"Look," I said, sitting down in a chair near my desk. "I need to ask a favor. I want to take Sare out for dinner this Friday—"

Bennett interrupted: "You're finally going to let someone watch Anna?"

Scowling, I explained, "It's a lot easier said than done, right? Anyway, Mum is leaving for Leeds tomorrow so she can't watch her this weekend. Can one of you . . . ?"

They both stared at me with terrified eyes.

"Aw come on, it's not that hard. We'd only go out for a few hours. You and your better half give her a couple of bottles, change a couple of diapers, she sleeps, we get home."

"We can't," Bennett said, wincing in apology. "Chloe and I are headed up to the Hudson Valley."

"This weekend?" Will asked, nodding several times in quick succession as if to talk himself into it. "I could probably do it."

"Brilliant," I said. "Thanks, mate."

"I've never changed a diaper. Or fed a baby. Hanna jokes that the only girl I've ever failed to charm is Liv's daughter, Aspen." Shrugging, he added, "But I'm sure it's instinct, right?" He ticked the rules off on his fingers: "Don't scald Anna in the bath, don't leave the milk in the microwave too long." He paused and seemed to continue to draft a mental list. "Oh, and don't drop her."

I imagined walking out of the office right now and leaving Annabel in Will's hands for even a minute; my stomach flipped over and I wanted to vomit. "Couldn't you bring Hanna?"

"She's got some visiting-faculty dinners this weekend."

Rubbing my hand across my chin, I asked, "You know . . . maybe you could come over and have dinner with us tonight to watch and learn?"

He nodded, but swallowed heavily. To be fair, I knew what I was asking was a big deal. It was one thing to hang out with us when we had Annabel, and quite another to imagine being alone with this tiny little girl.

"Can't you just take it to the restaurant with you?" Bennett asked.

"That sort of defeats the purpose. Also, Annabel isn't an 'it.'"

"I didn't call her an 'it.'"

Will and I replied in unison, "Yeah, you did."

Scrubbing my face, I muttered, "Fuck it. Just come over for dinner and we'll have some beers."

We'd figure something out. We had to.

Two

SARA

I turned down Fifty-Sixth and caught sight of the Parker Meridien near the end of the block.

The gray stone façade was as bleak as the morning sky; the clouds overhead fat with snow that was certain to start falling any minute. Winter in New York after Christmas was dreary: cold and wet, dirty slush, and days at a time without a hint of blue sky. But this year had been blessedly mild compared to others, and warm enough for Max to regularly push the bundled-up stroller alongside Will and Hanna as they ran through the park.

My phone buzzed in the front pocket of my coat. I didn't need to look to know it was Chloe, sending the third Where are you? You are not backing out on us Sara! message in the last hour. So maybe I'd missed a few lunches with the girls since Anna had been born, it wasn't easy getting out of the house with a newborn who would be permanently attached to my breast if given the chance.

I ignored my phone, my head still full of my morning with Max. Chloe could wait.

But of course only two steps later I was clutched with the fear that maybe the text hadn't been Chloe. Maybe it was Max with a message that Anna was sick or had hurt herself or—

I moved off the sidewalk to stand in the shelter of a nearby building, and pulled out my phone.

Will might come over for dinner, Max had written. You good with that?

I replied that it was fine and slid my phone back into my pocket. With each step, my favorite boots crunched through the salt that had been scattered along the sidewalk. Chloe wanted to take me shopping before I braved the office today, but I'd declined. I wanted the comfort of my favorite skirt and the heels that added just a little swing to my step, the sweater that rendered Max speechless and then *consumed* this morning. I needed to feel like myself.

I straightened my jacket and tightened my grip on the purse Max had bought me for my birthday. A Burberry clutch, not a diaper bag. I hadn't been out of the house without my baby, let alone diapers, bottles, wipes, and a change of clothes, since Anna was born, and the soft leather felt too light in my hand.

Just a few hours away from her today, I reminded myself. *Just see how it goes.*

~

I SMILED AT THE doorman as I stepped inside the marble lobby. The floors were gleaming white and inlaid with glossy black squares, the walls made of polished stone. People gathered on benches and sat hunched over their phones. Conversations carried through the giant space and up, echoing off stone walls. I walked under a giant arch and turned left, climbing a set of stairs that led to Norma's. As usual, I could hear Chloe before I could see her.

"There she is," Chloe said, standing on skyscraper-tall boots, all long legs and cascading wavy hair and an expression that said there was no way I'd get out of being late without getting a little shit for it first. "Fucking *finally*."

"I know, I know," I said, crossing the wood floors to reach them. "Sorry. Just trust me that time warps when you have a kid, and you think you're getting out of the house on time and then suddenly you're half an hour late."

"Are you sure it wasn't because Max saw you in that outfit and got a little handsy?" Hanna asked from beside Chloe.

"Spoken like a woman who's with a boob man," I said, laughing. "And . . . maybe."

I adored Hanna, but Max in particular had grown especially fond of her in the past year, saying that anyone who could keep Will Sumner by the balls was aces in his book.

"Just ignore Attila the Hun over here," my assistant and good friend George said, motioning to Chloe. "The woman isn't happy unless she's bossing someone around."

"Hell yes," Chloe said.

I hugged them all and hung my coat on the back of my chair before taking my seat.

"How's the princess?" Chloe said, blowing over the top of her mug. "*Where's* the princess?"

"Perfect. She's with Daddy today." A proud smile spread across my face. "How's the Bennett?"

"A nightmare," she answered, equally proud.

"And what's new with you and Will?" I asked, turning to Hanna. "I feel like I hardly see you, even if Max has taken it upon himself to crash your runs lately. Sorry about that."

Hanna leaned an elbow on the table and smiled. "I love when he comes along. And judging by the goofy look Will gets on his face when he sees that running stroller heading down the path, I can assure you he doesn't mind, either."

"Good, because as bad as I feel, the extra hour of sleep I get makes me feel a *lot* better."

"Maybe I should join those runs," George offered. "Does Will run shirtless in the spring?"

"George," Hanna said, ignoring this, "are you going to tell Sara about the little dreamboat you've been seeing?"

"*Was* seeing," he corrected. "As in past tense. Ugh, it was a stage-one breakup. I don't want to talk about it."

"A stage what?" Chloe asked.

"A *stage one*," he clarified. "I swear, do I always have to be the gay urban dictionary for you people? Stage one is where you break up via text message trying to come off not looking like a total douche bag. Stage two is where you tell the person, 'Look, you're not ringing my bell and I'm clearly not ringing yours. Let's move this train along to grander stations.' Stage three is where it's not working and you sort of fade the person out over time. It's painful because by then the other person has become sort of a habit. They know how you take your coffee and what days you can have carbs and just . . . it can be sad."

"Of course it can," I said. "Bonding over dietary restrictions can be very romantic."

George gave me a playful jab to the shoulder. "You get a sarcasm pass because you're lactating and it's clearly eating your brain. Where was I? Oh, stage four. Well . . . stage four is where one person is totally invested and the other is just . . . over it. Awful, right? So, stage one doesn't sound so bad, but in my opinion it's the worst after stage four. If someone feels comfortable breaking up via text message, you clearly haven't gotten to a place where you can ask a lot of questions, and you definitely can't call them up and be all *Oh hi, it's me, the guy you wore the Lion Tamer outfit with? Can you tell me what happened?*"

We all nodded sympathetically, and George glared at the bowl of muffins in the center of the table before reaching for one. "Now I'm eating my feelings."

"Aww, George. Were you totally infatuated with him?" Hanna asked.

"Oh, girl, no," George said with a laugh. "I don't do infatuation unless his name is Sumner."

The waiter stopped by our table, filling my coffee before taking each of our orders. "I'll have the crispy waffle with berries and Devonshire cream," I told him.

"I have no idea how you look like this," Chloe said, motioning to my body, "and still eat like that. You don't run with Hanna, and I know I haven't seen you at the office gym in months."

"One of the joys of breastfeeding," I said. "I have to eat more calories to keep up my milk."

Which was true. I still worked out when I could, but pregnancy and motherhood had left me with this new body I was only now getting used to: a slightly wider waist, but curves that had never been so full. I'd always been a bit on the skinny side, but I felt softer now, with rounded hips and boobs that surprised even me. It didn't hurt that sometimes I'd turn around and see Max flat-out staring at my chest, completely unable to look away. I'd be lying if I didn't say those moments made me feel like a fucking queen.

"What's the plan when you go back to work?" Hanna

asked, and taking in my outfit, added, "I'm assuming that's where you're headed now?"

I nodded as I took a sip of my coffee. "I don't officially go back until next week, but thought it might be easier to ease myself into it."

"Are you actually going to walk into your office and sit at your desk today?" George asked.

George had been a godsend while I was on leave. I was out for sixteen weeks, but I'd never wanted to feel disconnected from my career at Ryan Media Group, so I'd stop in on a pretty regular basis even though anything I needed to look at could have easily been couriered over to the apartment. Without really talking about it, we'd built up a system: Anna and I would meet George at his desk in the outer office, he'd hand me the stack of files and any messages that required my attention, and I'd leave him whatever I'd been working on at home.

I never went inside my office and he never questioned why.

Which was ridiculous, when you thought about it. I was Sara Stella, capable of managing multimillion-dollar campaigns and overseeing an entire finance department.

But I hadn't quite figured out how to do all that and be mommy, too.

"You haven't gone into your office yet?" Hanna asked. "Is it going to be weird to go back?"

"I don't think so? I mean, I want to go back to work. I

need to. It's such a part of who I am and I need that part of my life. But Anna . . . the idea of leaving her for eight hours a day still fills me with this guilt like I'm ruining her somehow or I'm missing some vital mommy muscle that makes me want to stay home. Plus, I know I want more at some point and how will we make all that work? Is it fair of me to want more children when I'm pretty sure I'll always need *that* side of me, too?"

"Bullshit," Chloe said. "You think men ever have this conversation with themselves? Of course they don't. You've killed yourself to get where you are. If you can have both, have both. It might take some adjustment but who cares? You figure it out as you go." She tilted her head and added, "You don't see Max wanting to stay home."

"Actually," I started, and it was enough to get Chloe's attention. She put down her mug and sat back in her chair, waiting. "I don't really know what's going on with him right now. I know he wants me every bit as much as he did before Anna, but I think it's been more of an adjustment for him than he thought it would be, the idea of my being a wife *and* a mother. He's so careful, like he's not sure how to treat me."

"Can you blame the man?" George said, and we all turned to him. "Have you seen what childbirth does to a vagina?" He did a full-body shudder.

"*George*," Chloe said, shaking her head.

"What!" he shouted.

"Shut up!" she shouted back.

"As horrible a flashback as that was," I said, "George has a point. I think Max is worried he'll do something to hurt me, and I'm not really sure how to show him I'm the same Sara I was before. That I *want* the same things I did before."

Chloe shrugged and picked up her coffee. "I don't know, Sara. He went from having you all to himself to watching you learn how to be a mama. Doesn't surprise me his brain is having to rewrite that code a little."

"I don't think it's about having to share me . . ." I hedged, but Chloe held up a hand.

"I mean it's about shifting how he sees you," she said, lifting an arched brow. "First you were the lust of his life, and now you're the mother of his daughter."

I chewed my lip, nodding. "He worries that I'm delicate now."

"Exactly," she said, a bit more gently. "Having Anna was traumatic. It wasn't as easy a birth as you both expected. You've already forgotten it, but maybe he hasn't and still needs to get over it."

Chloe was right. Sex this morning had been wild and hard, as if wanting me took over the part of Max's brain that told him to slow down. *That*'s what I wanted.

"When was the last time just the two of you went out?" George asked.

"Since Anna? We haven't."

It was his turn for a little eyebrow snark. "Well there's part of your problem right there, babycakes."

"Are we just talking wild sex here?" Chloe asked. "Because it's not like Annabel would have a clue what's going on."

"True," George said, "but it's probably a lot harder to fuck like wild animals with a baby asleep two doors down. You need a little space."

He had a point. "I love my baby more than anything in the world, but I want hours and hours. I want to bang my husband until he can't remember his name."

Silence bounced around the table for a few breaths.

"Too blunt?" I asked, laughing.

"Never," George said quickly. "I think we're all just working on that mental image."

"God, I sound desperate," I say, resting my chin on my fist. "Maybe we should just start with dinner out? I think Max is asking his mom if she can watch Anna this weekend."

"Otherwise next weekend Bennett and I can help," Chloe said.

"Whoa, whoa, whoa," George cut in. "What am I here for? My subtle charm? My pretty face? What about me?"

Chloe whipped her head around dramatically. "*You?*"

"I'll have you know that my mother ran a day care, and I taught preschool all through college. Hell, I worked in the infant room when I was in high school to pay for majorette class." Chloe went to respond but he held up a hand: "Shut it, Mills." He turned to me. "I'll watch Anna. I can even watch her tonight."

"You'd watch her?" I asked. "You could really do that?"

"With my eyes closed. Besides," he said, eyeing the muffins again, "it's not like I have any kind of social life to speak of. My nights are wide open."

∽

THE SMELL OF HOME hit me before I'd even walked in the door. My talk with the girls and George had done wonders, and I'd successfully navigated the day with no freak-outs, no tears, and only one breast milk incident when a phone call went long and I couldn't get to my pump in time. Next time, I'd just do it while I was on the phone. Boom. My friends were right; I'd figure it out as I went.

Basically, I was feeling pretty unstoppable as I rounded the corner, ready to tell Max about our dinner that night. Then I found him shirtless—again—wrapped in nothing but a towel, with a tiny sleeping baby in his arms, and I was ready to forget about dinner entirely and let him get me pregnant again that very second.

Focus, Sara.

"Tell Will I'm sorry, but you're busy tonight."

Max looked up at me. "About that, he sends his apologies, but something came up." A moment of silence passed before he realized what I'd said. "And I am?"

"Yep. I'm taking you to dinner," I said. "Surprise! Also, I can't believe I'm saying this, but I'm going to need you to put some clothes on for real this time or we'll never get out of the apartment."

Max looked up, confused. "Dinner? How did you—?" Sitting up, he said, "And no, I meant to ring you today. I wanted to take you to dinner this weekend but Mum is leaving for Leeds tomorrow. I completely forgot it was in my schedule."

"That's what I'm saying: *George* is watching Anna *tonight*."

"Tonight? Has George ever even seen a baby?"

I crossed the room and kissed him softly on the mouth. "Hi," I said, and kissed him again. "I know what you're thinking, but it's perfect." I took the sleeping baby from his arms and leaned in, pressing my face to her soft little head, breathing in as much of her as I could. She had Max's hair for sure, only a shade darker than mine but already with a bit of a wave to it. Her clean-baby smell hit me, and I felt my breasts grow heavy, my milk letting down almost immediately.

A chair Max brought me from England sat tucked beneath the window in the nursery. It was my favorite place in the apartment, where I was able to look out over the city while I nursed. I got Anna situated, and then looked up at him.

He clearly thought I'd lost my mind. "Are we talking about the same George?"

"I had breakfast with everyone this morning before I

went in to work. Did you know that George's mom ran a day care while he was growing up? He worked there while he was in high school and all through college. He worked with *infants*."

He gave me his best skeptical face. "We're talking about the same twenty-something bloke who wore a Wisconsin cheese hat and some flowy Jesus robes for Halloween, calling himself 'Cheesus'?"

"The one and only," I said, laughing at the memory. "He's probably more qualified to take care of her than we are. Plus we'll stay close. Just around the corner. He can text or call with any questions and we can be back up here in less than three minutes."

"But . . ."

"No buts. This is exactly what we need. Now get dressed, he'll be here in fifteen minutes."

GEORGE SHOWED UP EXACTLY fourteen minutes later.

From the bathroom, I could hear Max open the door and let him in, and begin grilling him as they went from room to room.

"And what about her bottle?" Max asked, clearly hoping to be proven right, and that George had absolutely no idea what he was doing.

"Sara's breastfeeding so I assume you have expressed

milk in the freezer? Maybe even fresh in the refrigerator," George said, more to himself than to Max, I was sure. "What am I talking about? Honestly, I think I've seen more of Sara's boobs in the last four months than my own." There was the sound of the refrigerator door as it opened and closed, and I stepped out into the living room, watching as George answered Max's questions one by one. Max looked begrudgingly impressed.

"I assume she's getting about six ounces a feeding," George continued. "Probably every three hours or so? I'll heat the refrigerated milk first—only ever under warm water, never the microwave. It kills beneficial properties, you know—and I'll use the frozen if needed. Though you'll probably be back by then . . ." George trailed off.

"We have a bottle warmer," Max said, brow furrowed in what I was certain had to be confusion. George really did seem to be more knowledgeable about taking care of an infant than we were. "And nappies?"

"You mean diapers? Oh you Brits are so damn cute. And please, Maxwell. I could probably diaper you in your sleep and you'd never have any idea. I am a pro."

"Or so you've been told," I said, stepping out to kiss his cheek. "Sorry, Chloe's not here and I had to throw that in for her. Thank you so much for doing this."

He waved me off. "No problem. The little princess and I will probably just sit here and cry through *The Notebook*. For very, very different reasons, I'm sure."

Between kisses and cuddles and last-minute instructions, it took another fifteen minutes for George to shoo us out of the apartment.

༄

BUT WE DIDN'T GO to the restaurant around the corner. George had apparently made such an impression that Max made us last-minute reservations at a little Italian place a few miles away. I was nervous at the prospect of leaving Anna when I didn't have to, but I was also giddy. We were going on a *date*, just the two of us, and my pulse hadn't slowed down yet.

I watched his profile as he drove us to the restaurant; as I studied the way the streetlights passing overhead emphasized the fullness of his lips, the cut of his jaw, I thought back to our first real *date*—is that what that was?—when he'd taken me to Queen of Sheba and I hadn't been able to stop looking at his mouth. I *still* couldn't stop looking at his mouth.

The press didn't follow him like they did before we were together, but since Anna had been born, there was an uptick in Hot Daddy Max Stella photos in Page Six and on various Internet gossip sites. I couldn't say that I blamed them, no matter how much I still resented them for ever spooking me in the first place.

I closed my eyes, my heart squeezing tightly as I was

pulled back in time to our first night together after the pictures in the papers, the ones that made me think he'd cheated. He'd thrown a party, and after not answering his calls for over a week, I'd shown up, finally ready to talk. But it hadn't been as simple as I'd expected—he'd been genuinely hurt—and I'd had some apologizing to do.

I remembered the small, grudging smile Max gave me when we woke up together the next morning; he had handed over the last tiny bit of himself with that.

I remembered how that look had squeezed my heart, painfully. He'd been scared to let me back in, and in the stark white light of the morning, with both of us sweaty and spent, we couldn't hide with our faces pressed to the other's skin, or in the game of transparency through photos. He looked at me directly, baldly, and there was nothing else between us.

"Stay," he said, bending to suck at the skin just beneath my ear. "Stay with me. It's good, Petal. *Us*. It's so sodding good and if you spook again it will absolutely wreck me."

"I won't."

"I love you, yeah?"

I nodded, heart trapped somewhere between my throat and the sky. "I love you."

"That means we're settled. It means there's no question where my heart is. You'll stay here."

It had been that easy. It had always been that easy. And I had learned to trust it.

But now it was a different shape: bigger, yes, but unwieldy, and the ease of it all—Max and Sara, a rhythm ricocheting between us like a shared heartbeat—was now pounding too hard for me to bear.

Because now I felt *everything*. It was like a faucet had been turned on inside me, filling me with warmth and pride and thrill and terror and vulnerability and strength and powerlessness and lust and it never shut off. It filled and filled until I was sure I was bursting from it, but how could I ever complain that I felt too much? How could I explain that I was burning up with the constant awareness that if anyone ever tried to hurt my man or my baby I would rip them inside out with my rage?

How could I ever complain that it was often hard to find myself in the desire to be mother and lover in equal measure to the two people in my life who seemed to matter above even my own need for air?

Max held my hand as we drove, until a text from George pulled me out of my memories.

"Aww," I said, turning the screen to face him. It was a picture of Anna asleep on George's shoulder, her fat little fist pressed against her perfect mouth.

"Maybe we should send him flowers next week to thank him," Max said, and then I recognized the little twist in his smile that signaled he was up to no good. "And say they're from Will."

"Don't you dare," I told him, saving the picture before

tucking my phone away. "If this works out we're going to use him again. Hell, I might just change his job position from assistant to nanny and offer him a raise."

"I might have to let you," he said, and brought the back of my hand to his mouth for a kiss. "Maybe then I can sneak you away for a weekend? Someplace we can lock ourselves in our room the entire time, not a stitch of clothing on either of us?"

"That sounds pretty close to perfect."

My phone buzzed in my clutch, and we stopped long enough for me to reach for it, unsurprised to find another text from George.

Look how gorgeous she is!! it said, along with a photograph of Anna fast asleep in her crib and several heart-eyed emojis.

"This is way too easy," I told Max. "But instead of questioning it, I'm going to put this away and enjoy the hell out of this night. And maybe if you're lucky, I'll let you have your way with me on the way home."

"That, Petal, is the most amazing thing I've heard all day." Max curved his hand around the back of my neck and pulled me to him. I went willingly, my mind already spinning ahead to what could happen after dinner, where we might go and the delightfully filthy things he might do to me. This is what we'd been missing. Max and Sara. Tonight was absolutely perfect.

Max pulled up to the valet at Granduca's and an attendant reached for my door. "I've got it, mate," he said, rounding the car and offering a hand to help me out.

Mindful of the fact that I was in a dress, I carefully swung my feet out onto the ground and moved to stand. Max's hand felt warm and reassuring in my own and I took a step, intending to follow him into the restaurant. But I couldn't.

What the . . . I almost gasped when I realized that I was stuck. Or to be more accurate, that my *dress* was. The subtle beading on my skirt had snagged on the inside door latch of Max's BMW.

"I'm just . . ." I started, letting go of Max in an attempt to get a better look. "My dress seems to be caught."

Max kneeled next to me but I waved him off.

"No, just one second, let me."

By now the attendant with Max's keys had realized something was wrong, and so had a few of the others. "Maybe if you try and slip that piece right there through the latch," one of them said.

"No, that will make it worse. See those little beads? They'll get stuck. I've got some scissors. I can go grab them," said another.

"Man, it is really *in* there," said their supervisor. "How did you even do that?"

Four pairs of hands all tried to help me untangle myself, but I batted them away.

"No," I said. "Please. This dress is vintage." There was a grimace in my voice as I pulled on a tiny thread, careful not to snag it further. Damn, it did not want to give and I was practically sweating. "A gift from my mom," I added. "Just let me—"

"Oh," they all said in unison, along with a "Fucking hell," from Max.

I'd ripped it, like, *really* ripped it. And now, instead of a small, easily concealable snag, there was a slit that began at the bottom of my skirt and moved up, stopping at the top of my thigh.

"No way that just happened," Max said.

"It happened," I told him.

"I'm sorry, Petal. We can go back and you can change into something else?"

"This is nothing," I said, and straightened, pushing up on the balls of my feet to press a kiss to his neck. "This is just karma's way of proving a point because I said this was too easy. *Of course* something would go wrong after that."

"I'd be lying if I said that I disliked this slight alteration," he said, eyes moving up and down my thigh.

"It's not too obscene?" I asked, a little thrill passing through my stomach at his wide eyes as he shook his head.

"Absolutely not." He ran his hand down over my hip, and touched the bare skin of my thigh, right in front of everyone outside the restaurant.

Warmth slid into my veins. Was he going to play a little tonight? Would he touch me beneath the table?

"Listen," he said, kissing my neck, "why don't I check

us in and you can run to the ladies', fix anything that needs fixing and maybe check in on George?"

I wilted immediately. "Sounds perfect," I said, squeezing his hand.

I didn't call George, opting to text instead of running the risk of waking Anna.

I know I don't need to check in so just saying hi. Hi, I typed.

His reply came less than a minute later. If you two aren't naked yet I'm going to be so disappointed.

I laughed dryly as I typed back, Nope, definitely not naked. How's my baby?

Perfect. Just waking up so I'm heating her bottle. Then tummy time and a movie.

You're a lifesaver, I typed.

Tell me something I don't know.

I looked at the full-length mirror in the ladies' room and Max was right, it didn't look bad at all. Satisfied, I left to go find my husband, typing out a response on the way. How will I ever repay you, George?

Bring me back something shiny.

I smiled. Done.

By shiny, you know I mean chorus boys wrapped in sparkling swim trunks, right?

Obviously.

His response appeared only a second later. This is why we're friends.

WE WERE LED TO our seats shortly after. With the way Max was looking at me from across the table—like nothing would please him more than to spread me out in front of all these people and have *me* for dinner—I hoped I'd be able to make it through the next two hours.

I opted for clam risotto with bacon and chives, and Max ordered a creamy fettuccine with asparagus. The waiter brought a bottle of pinot noir and held it out for Max's inspection. Max smiled and then motioned for him to show it to me—which was ridiculous considering I barely drank—but my eyes widened in recognition. It was the same wine we'd had at the quiet dinner after our wedding at city hall. My husband was *so* getting laid tonight.

"Perfect," I told him.

The waiter smiled and began to remove the cork. "It's an amazing choice," he said, wedging the bottle between his knees to get a better grip. He laughed nervously and jostled the opener, but it didn't seem to want to budge. "Wow, it's really stuck in there."

"Maybe if I—" Max started to say, but the cork came out with a wet suction and both the waiter and Max eyed it dubiously. It was black with sludge.

"Oh," both the waiter and I said in unison. Max looked like someone had just popped his balloon.

"This is a pretty bleak metaphor," I joked, but Max's expression told me he didn't think it was remotely funny.

"I'm so sorry," the waiter said, and looked around as if someone would be standing there to help him. "This bottle is clearly off. I'll just go get you another." He paused, and I knew right away that it wasn't a good sign. "I just remembered, that was the last one."

"No worries, mate," Max said, glancing through the wine menu. "Happens to all of us. We'll just have a bottle of the MacRostie instead."

～

The wine had been poured, and I tore off a small piece of warm bread while we waited for our meal. "So how was Anna today?" I asked.

Max looked at me over the rim of his glass, mouth turned up in a teasing smirk. "I believe there was to be no baby discussion tonight, Mrs. Stella," he said. "But since I relish the chance to talk about our daughter, I'll tell you that she was perfect, as usual. Mum quite enjoys having her there. Not to mention Will, even if he does nothing more than sit and make ridiculous faces at her from across the table."

As if on cue, my phone vibrated next to my plate and I glanced over as the screen lit up.

Your daughter is not impressed with Ryan Gosling.

This is clearly your husband's DNA. Attached was a photo of the two of them on the couch, Anna making a hilariously frowny face at the camera.

I showed Max and typed out a quick reply, before placing my phone—facedown—on the table.

Max reached for my hand and took it in his, rubbing his thumb over my wedding band. "It's okay to look at your phone, you know. This is our first night out without her. It's all right to feel a little anxious. *I'm* a little anxious."

"You don't look it," I told him. "You never do. I swear you have a poker face like nothing I've ever seen."

"I don't know about that. Seems I couldn't keep anything from you, now could I? Quite certain you knew I was ass over tits for you within a few days of meeting."

"You played the rogue part pretty well, though. Even I—" My phone vibrated again and I bit back a groan.

It was more movie commentary from George, and honestly, if the accompanying pics weren't so adorable and I didn't love him so much for doing this for me, I'd probably offer to buy him a car to lose my number for the next forty-five minutes.

Has Anna been fussier than usual? Or doing this thing where she pulls her body up into a little bit before kicking out and crying?

"Was Anna fussy today?" I asked Max, suddenly worried that I'd missed something being away.

"Maybe a tad more toward the end of the day, but nothing big. Was just ready to go home, that's all."

Not that we've noticed, I typed. Why? Is she ok?

I'm sure it's nothing, came George's reply. Her tummy feels a bit noisy to me, so I'm going to do a little baby massage on her. See if we can get all those gas bubbles gone.

"She's not feeling well," I told Max. "I mean, he thinks it's just gas but, I don't know."

"Would you feel better if we left, Petal?" he said, concern growing in his features.

"I don't know." I didn't, I wasn't sure if this was one of those moments where I needed to tell the overprotective side of myself to calm down, or give in to the worry pressing on my chest. A baby cried from somewhere near the back of the restaurant and I squeezed my eyes closed. Of course this would happen now. I could already feel the way my breasts felt heavier, tender. My milk was beginning to let down and I had no baby, no pump anywhere in sight. The night was going downhill, and fast.

Movement caught my eye, and I felt my shoulders sag with relief as I saw the waiter coming toward us with our dinners.

"Thank fuck," Max said. "Shall I get them to go?"

The phone buzzed on the table again, so close to my cutlery that it caused a shrill clanking as they vibrated against each other. As he set my plate down, the waiter gave me a look.

So baby girl feels better now, the text said. Unfortunately, she feels better because she threw up all over me. And your couch. It fought the good fight though.

"She threw up, all over George's fancy Italian shirt. Maybe send chocolates *and* flowers," I said. "And let's definitely get it all to go."

There are moments when you definitely know life has a sense of humor, when you swear that someone is up there screwing with you. My phone went off again, sending my silverware clanging across the table. I reached for it as the waiter picked Max's plate back up, at the *exact same moment* the person next to us stood, pushing out their chair. I grabbed for my phone, the chair collided with the waiter, and Max's plate of white cream sauce went tumbling . . . into his lap.

Water was everywhere, across the tablecloth and all over Max's pants, where a wet, creamy mixture now lay steaming. I scrambled back from the chaos, my eyes wide with horror. A child next to us burst into tears, and I looked over at Max and the enormous mess in his lap.

"It's fine," he assured me, grabbing a napkin and wiping his pants.

My phone buzzed on the table with another picture from George.

"It's okay, Petal. Just leave it."

I sat down, shaking. "This is a disaster. I just want to get home to my baby." I paused as Max dabbed at his pants again and looked down at my chest, my neck and cheeks flushing with humiliation, "Oh, *shit*."

When Max looked up and realized my milk had let down and soaked through my red dress, creating two big, wet circles, I could tell he was *done*.

Tossing a few twenties onto the table, he stood and helped me up, wrapping me in his coat. "Let's go home."

I tucked into his side and strode beside him quickly, wordlessly, until we got outside, where I couldn't help but start laughing madly. "We could have had cereal for dinner in our pajamas!"

"Fucking too right," he growled, handing the valet the ticket for our car. Protectiveness and frustration rolled off him in waves. "Giant bowl of Froot Loops and—"

"Sir," the valet interrupted, glancing at the number. His face was ashen. "Our deepest apologies, but I need to let you know there's been a slight accident . . ."

Three

MAX

I could hear Anna crying from the elevator and immediately knew George hadn't been able to get her to take a bottle.

Sara took off, running to the door and fumbling with her keys before I was able to take them from her and let her in. Just inside, George handed her the baby and—correctly reading Sara's expression—insisted, "She's okay, she's okay, she just woke up and wouldn't take the bottle. She had one earlier."

It wouldn't matter to know that she'd eaten not long before. Sara thanked George in a panicked whisper and took the baby into the nursery to feed her.

"Did you have an accident?" George nodded to my pants.

I looked away from where Sara had disappeared down the hall. "A waiter did, just before Sara had one, just before the valet introduced my car to a concrete pillar."

"So dinner was awesome, then?"

"A brilliant night, really." Only when I looked up at him again did I register what he was wearing. "Is that my shirt?"

George ran his hands to his hips. "It's more of a dress on me." He pulled the extra material into his fists. "I almost used one of Sara's scarves as a belt."

"So . . . a touch of vomit then?"

He nodded, releasing the shirt. "Exorcist baby."

"Sorry about that," I mumbled, suddenly hit with a debilitating wave of exhaustion. "I swear there are times she throws up more than I think she's eaten."

"Not a thing, I swear. It was so much better than that time my date threw up on me, because at least Anna cuddles afterward."

"Thanks, mate. Taking care of the baby tonight was bloody generous of you."

George patted my shoulder. "I'll leave you to it. Tell Sara I'll see her next week?"

"Will do."

After I closed the door behind him, I threw my trousers in the washing machine and went down the hall to the nursery, sitting in my usual spot on the soft carpet near the rocking chair. "How's my girl?"

Sara smiled down at Anna. "She's fine."

I licked my lips, studying her face. She'd relaxed almost as soon as she had our baby in her arms. "I meant my wife."

Her enormous brown eyes met mine and narrowed as she laughed. "I'm fine, too."

She looked back down at the baby and sang quietly, stroking Anna's cheek with her thumb. I watched Anna's small hand reach up blindly, finding and squeezing Sara's index finger. Reaching forward, I curled my hand around my wife's ankle and closed my eyes.

I couldn't hear anything but Sara's quiet humming and our daughter's little baby noises. Our world was infinitely better and we had to come to terms with the fact that, at least for the time being, it was so much smaller.

❧

A HAND ON MY shoulder startled me awake. The floor of the nursery, I'd fallen asleep on the floor of the nursery . . .

Looking up, I was greeted by the sight of Sara in a tiny lace bra that pushed her tits up and together until they nearly spilled from the cups. My gaze traveled south and snagged on her minuscule matching thong.

"New pajamas?" I asked, pushing up onto an elbow.

"A gift from Chloe."

"For me or you?"

"Both." She curled her finger to me as she backed out of the room, and I stood, trailing after her until she stopped halfway to the bedroom on a slim, soft hallway rug.

"Here?" I asked, stepping close and bending to kiss her neck. She'd put the smallest touch of perfume on—the familiar light scent that seemed half fruit, half floral, and which she knew made me wild. Seeing her like this, in lingerie, her hair grown long and thick, reaching halfway down her back and brushed smooth, reminded me that it had been forever since we'd put in this sort of effort. It used to be either frantic fucking or a luxurious game.

Now we'd only known exhausted or frantic, and I couldn't shake the feeling that I should take her to our room, be slow and gentle with her.

"Yeah, here," she whispered, standing on her toes to scrape her teeth over my jaw. "Remember that time we ate dinner in front of the TV, and I surprised you when the movie I put in was a video of us?" She dragged her teeth along my earlobe. "You got so turned on you fucked me against this wall. Bent at the waist, hands on the plaster and legs spread? Remember?"

I definitely remembered. We'd made love in the hall before—the frantic kind of pre-baby sex when we'd been unable to wait until we could reach the bed. Those times were fast and messy, a flurry of wild thrusts until we both collapsed sweaty and half dressed on the floor. On that particular occasion I'd just watched a video of me spanking her, and was so fucking turned on we re-created it, right here.

But tonight, when Annabel was fast asleep, why were we—

"I like this rug," she explained, sliding down my body to her knees and my brain stuttered when she looked up at me with wicked eyes. "It's soft and thick under my knees." She guided my boxers down past my hips and freed my cock, watching it grow long as her fist curled around the base. She drew a slow circle with her tongue around the tip. "I also like the way you taste," she continued, smiling knowingly up at me. "Is that weird?"

I opened my mouth, searching for sound, and finally grunted out a "No."

She bit her lip, watching her fist work me for a few strokes before sucking at the crown again. I groaned, tensing from the pleasure of her swirling tongue. "I like this sweetness," she whispered and stared up at me. "Relax. Tonight was a disaster, but a *funny* disaster. Give me more."

Sara squeezed me, coaxing liquid from the tip and sucking at it. "What's it like to watch me do that?"

My mouth opened and I tried to speak but only a garbled sound came out. Her tongue rubbed across the spot just beneath the head of my cock and my hand tightened on the back of her neck, breath tight and high in my throat.

Popping off with a wet kiss she asked, "When was the last time you came in my mouth?"

I knew the answer without having to think too long. It was two weeks after the baby was born and we couldn't have sex yet. We were delirious with sleep deprivation and on some sort of high over the perfection of our lives anyway. I came on her lips not because she played with me for so long, but because we hadn't touched intimately in several weeks and I'd felt spring-loaded.

"A while ago," I admitted.

She nodded, lips pouting before she smiled and bent to kiss a wet, sucking line up my cock.

I wanted her hands around me, gripping and pulling, frenzied in that way that we seemed to never have energy for anymore. Wanted that slick slide of tongue over my skin and the vibrating sounds of pleasure, the urgency. She bent, licking another wet line from the head to my balls, smiling with her eyes up at me as she pointed her tongue and ran it around and around and around in a wet circle at the very tip of my cock.

Fuck.

My fingers found their way into her hair, massaging, guiding her down and I was speaking nonsense; encouraging her and begging her and praising her fucking perfect, sweet little mouth.

"Love that mouth. Fucking *love* it." I ran a finger down from her temple to her lips, feeling her slide back and forth over me. "I bet you could take me all the way down, couldn't you?" I said, giving in to what I wanted so *so* much.

She took me farther and farther until her eyes watered and she pulled back, sucking in air and staring up at me. I was harder than I'd been in ages, practically shaking with the need for her.

I needed Sara's deep brown eyes and quiet, scratchy voice and hands that were both soft and strong. I wanted only the arch of Sara's spine and the taste of the wet between her legs and the clench of her when she came around me with a shocked cry. I'd been with her a hundred times and every one of those times she'd been a different woman—a new discovery—revealing something new of herself.

With my cock between her lips, she reached back and unfastened her bra, letting it slide down her arms and land silently on the floor.

Her eyes twinkled as she looked up at me and when she reached forward and played with her nipple, I was fucking done.

Perfect suction, her hot little ass in perfect view . . . *holy fuck*. I closed my eyes and gave in to the clawing ache that built in my thighs and stretched upward, tightening . . .

A tiny thump sounded in the other room: Anna rolling into the side of the crib. She coughed a few times.

I started to step away but Sara planted her hands on my hips with quiet urgency. "She's fine. You're so close, baby, *stay*."

And then the baby started to cry.

Sara slid her mouth down again, sucking hard and fast, begging with her eyes for me to relax, to come, to keep this moment alive somehow, but how the bloody hell was I supposed to fuck her mouth with our infant daughter crying in the other room?

The hungry cry, Sara once told me. *"Do you hear it?"* she'd asked. *"How different it sounds?"*

I knew without having to even ask that her breasts were growing heavy and uncomfortable.

This time, when I stepped back, she let me.

I ran the pad of my thumb from her temple down across her cheek to rest on her full, wet bottom lip. "Petal. Go on."

With an apologetic grimace she took my hand and stood. She looked so fucking beautiful in front of me: topless, wearing her tiny lace pants, legs toned and smooth. She stretched and kissed me once, soft and slow, trapping my cock between us.

"We'll finish this later?"

"Sure," I murmured, kissing her forehead.

Her ass, when she turned and stepped into the nursery, was sublime. And then she bent, picked up our baby, and walked to the rocking chair.

Instead of sitting at her feet like usual, I went down the hall into the bedroom to let my body come down.

Twenty minutes later I felt Sara crawl into bed behind me. Her hand was warm when it slid around my chest. Her mouth was soft and wet on the bare skin of my shoulder.

"You awake?" she whispered, letting her hand run down my stomach to where I was naked under the covers. My body began to respond when she gripped me, but I was so fucking close to sleep, so exhausted. I took her hand in mine and pulled it up to my chest, wordlessly telling her we'd find another time.

"Good morning, sunshine." Will was sitting in my office guest chair, his feet perched on my desk.

I glanced at him and then shut my office door behind me. "Comfortable?"

"My office is better," he said in response. "How was the epic shagfest?"

"Mildly disappointing."

His playful expression dimmed at my probably-too-honest answer and he sat up, planting his elbows on his knees. "What happened?"

I dropped my laptop bag near my office closet and sat across from him. "George was good, it was just a lot of updates, a lot of mishaps at the restaurant, and then the sex that never quite happened after."

"What kind of mishaps?"

"Alfredo on the trousers, water dumped on the mix, Sara's breasts leaking through her dress, the valet scraped my car. You know, the usual date night."

Will held up a hand. "Her breasts and the dress and the *what* now?"

I sighed. "William. Sometimes you disappoint me with your predictability."

But he was already shaking his head. "I'm honestly curious. They . . . *leak*?"

I felt my brows pull together. "Well . . . yeah. 'Course they do. You do realize where milk comes from, right?

What they're actually for? That they weren't created simply for you to enjoy."

"Do *not* blaspheme, Max," he said, holding out a single finger in warning. He looked a little dazed. "And they leak like, *constantly*?"

"Not constantly, you bleeding idiot. Just when she hasn't fed Anna in a few hours or if she hears her cry . . ." I winced, meeting his eyes. "Or another baby cry, apparently. I didn't really anticipate that one, to be honest."

I didn't know what to say. It wasn't that I felt like I was betraying Sara's privacy in talking about this; it was more that I felt I had access to a secret room in the man tavern and I really shouldn't hand over the password to Will until it was his time. Let him suffer a bit.

I gave him my most condescending smile. "Lots of things happen with the female body that even you haven't seen."

He rolled his eyes. "Don't patronize me."

"Why?" I clucked my tongue sympathetically. "It brings me such joy."

Will tilted his head, and seemed to consider whether or not to tell me something. His blue eyes narrowed and a little smile took over one half of his mouth.

I waited it out until I knew he couldn't stand it anymore. The staring contest continued for at least ten seconds longer.

"Fine," he said on a bursting exhale. "I've been with a pregnant woman before."

I regarded him with mild disgust. "Okay, given that I know you've never impregnated anyone yourself, I'm just going to say it: that's slightly fucking weird."

"Yeah . . . I did a lot of shit then that I wouldn't do now. But I've never been with a woman who . . ." He glanced down to his chest and looked back up at me, brows raised.

"Right," I said, rubbing the back of my neck. Will was such a notorious breast man, it occurred to me that it was strange that he hadn't seemed to think about this perk of motherhood before now.

"What does it taste like?" he said, like a crack in the air.

I groaned, rubbing my eyes. "William."

"*Maximillian.* Don't even try to pretend like you haven't tasted it."

I remembered the conversation Sara and I had about it the first week we were home. We were in the newborn haze, with dishes piled in the sink and in the same clothes we'd worn the day before. Sara was in pain, and I did what I could to help relieve it: with my hands, my mouth. She'd watched, eyes wide and grateful, her nails gently scratching my scalp and asked me how it tasted.

I blinked back over to Will. "It's . . . sweet," I admitted.

He whimpered, closing his eyes. "I feel like I need to meet Hanna at the apartment for a lunchtime—"

"Christ, you're pathetic."

He opened his eyes and studied me, eyes narrowing. "You dig it."

"Her tits are glorious. Of *course* I dig them."

"Not just that. *It*." He leaned forward, forcing me to hold his gaze. "You do! Holy shit! You dig that they leak and think it's weird. Are you feeling shame, Gentle Giant?"

I pulled back, shaking my head at him. "Absolutely not."

"And by 'absolutely not' you mean, 'I am absolutely horrified that I dig the—'"

"I'm close to kicking you out of my office."

He laughed, rocking the chair back on two legs. "Which means I'm close to unearthing the truth."

"The *truth*, you sodding wanker, is it's just a weird balance right now." I hesitated for a moment, trying to organize my thoughts. "Yes, of course there are things about it that are surprisingly hot. But before, it was just *us*. Max and Sara, living together, still getting to know each other. It's like you and Hanna now: you can stay out as late as you want, fuck as loud and often as you want, go on a weekend holiday without notice. We were deep in the throes of that, and now there is a little girl in my life who is more important than anything. And . . ." I pulled at the back of my neck. "I didn't expect it. I didn't expect to feel so many things at once. I feel like I'm walking around with my heart outside my body, and I know it's even more true for Sara. I didn't know how hard it would be to see her energy split.

So yeah, the fact that I basically want to fuck her all the time but worry that I'll . . ."

He sat quietly, listening. But when I couldn't figure how else to explain the strange tension in me, he guessed: "You feel guilty."

"A bit." I slid my palm across my mouth. "I mean, look. There's only so much I'm needed for right now. Sara feeds her, holds her. Anna wants her mum, you know? I can change her and sing to her and take her running, but she doesn't need *me* yet." I grimaced, hating how it sounded to admit: "But I still need a lot. It feels selfish to want the 'epic shagfest'—as you so delicately put it—to be just as wild as it ever was. It isn't just about me anymore."

"Funny that you haven't mentioned what *Sara* wants it to be like."

I groaned. "She wants me to be a bit rougher again, I think."

He stilled across the desk. "What the fuck is the problem? You two are on the same page, you asshat." Will leaned in, expression deliberately neutral. "You still doing . . . the club thing? At Johnny's?"

I'd always wondered how much Will really knew. Apparently, he knew quite a lot.

"We haven't in a long time," I admitted quietly, "not since she was pregnant. She wants to go."

"But you don't?" he asked, surprised.

"You fancy the idea of people watching you with Hanna?"

He started to nod, and then paused. "Yes, and no. I like the idea of people watching me unravel her, but I don't really want men fantasizing about her like that."

"See, and I don't mind that aspect. But take your feelings, and now imagine when Hanna's had your baby," I said. "When she's a nursing mum, and tired all the time and tiny the way Sara is. Yes, I fucking love her body right now but it all feels private and like if the world pushed her too hard I would break it in half with my bare hands. That it might break *her*. It didn't occur to me to feel like this when she was pregnant because there was nothing vulnerable about her, even when she was ready to pop. She carried herself like she knew she looked amazing. Now, if someone didn't appreciate how sexy she is, I would put my boot up their arse and kick out their teeth."

Will regarded me blandly and pretended to yawn.

"So you think this is me being over-fucking-protective."

"Like a *dick*," he said. "Like you said, this is your kink. It may not be mine, but if Sara likes it, why do you think it has to be different just because you have a baby at home?"

I leaned back in my chair, shook my head at him. "This is a pretty intense heart-to-heart we're having. Breast milk, kink, marriage, and sex with children in the mix. Can you handle it? When did you become a man, William?"

"Ha. This is nothing compared to some of the shit Hanna wants to talk about," he said and then laughed. "I mean, look. Anna is four months old. You know when you go to a matinee and come out and it's still light out and you're blinded and disoriented for about five seconds until your photoreceptors—"

"*Will*. Fucking focus."

"What I'm saying is, you're still stuck in those first five seconds. You've walked out of the building and have no idea what it looks like outside yet."

"Right. Good metaphor."

"You want to see some of your life you recognize. You want barely-inside-the-door sex. You want breaking-furniture sex. You want club sex. *And* you want to do it with those amazing tits."

I gnawed my lip and then admitted, "Right."

"Let us watch the kiddo. We're her godparents, right?" He held up a hand, keeping me from answering. "I mean, I know you haven't decided yet, but we'd be way better than Chloe and Bennett because let's be real: they're assholes."

I burst out laughing. "Bennett knows kids, though. He has a niece."

"He's terrified of newborns. Henry says he held Sophia at arm's length until she could walk and then he never let her out of his sight. He's sure he'll break Anna with a stern glance. Which I don't doubt, if I'm being honest. He is scary as hell sometimes. Hanna and I . . . we'll figure it out." Leaning forward, he winked. "We're *scientists*."

Four

SARA

For all the ways that Max, Bennett, and Will were alike, there were even more ways they were different. Bennett's first instinct was *always* to take charge, to work out the quickest way to get the upper hand and never let go. Max was the charmer—still one hell of a businessman, but a bowl of sugar—the guy who knew you caught more flies with honey than vinegar. But Will was the thinker, the one who would puzzle out a situation and figure out exactly what the problem was so he could fix it. Which was why when Max suggested that Will and Hanna watch Anna while we attempted Dinner Disaster number two, I agreed. Will and Hanna were two of the smartest people I knew; if anyone could figure out how to crack the baby code, it was them.

We were both ready to go when they showed up at the apartment the next Friday night.

Will was wearing a T-shirt from some show I'd never

heard of, and a wary expression on his face. Hanna—as usual—seemed to be getting a kick out of his nerves.

"You're not scared of a tiny little baby now, are you?" she asked as they stepped inside.

"Of course I'm not," Will said, unwrapping a blue scarf from around his neck. "But between eight and forty percent of babies get colic, Hanna. Eight and *forty* percent. That's almost half on the high end, and if you factor that into the number of babies born every year, then the chances that Annabel has—"

"She isn't colicky, you twat," Max said, pulling him in far enough that he could close the door. "Hanna, I hope he's at least brilliant with your taxes or at the very least one hell of a shag."

"Both, actually," she said, and handed Max her jacket. "And don't worry, I babysat a ton growing up. Probably watched every kid in the neighborhood at some point. I'm really great with babies."

Will stepped up to her side, leaned in to wrap his arms around her and press a small kiss to her nose. "How is that even possible when you were so busy pining for me?" he asked, grinning.

Hanna shook her head and patted Will's face gently. "It's so cute how you think everything's about you," she said, and Max barked out a laugh. Will was our notorious womanizer, and to see that he had finally met the woman who knocked him on his ass was amazing.

"Thank you, again, you guys," I said, pushing Will away so I could hug Hanna. "I'm not even sure optimism is the way to go, so I guess I'll just wish you luck."

"Don't be silly," Will said. "We—and by 'we' of course I mean Hanna—will take care of everything. I'm just here to open jars, kill spiders, and change lightbulbs if needed."

Hanna nodded.

Still, I made sure they knew where everything was, went over a list of emergency numbers, and then thanked them for what had to be the tenth time. "She's just eaten and been changed. I'm sure she'll be good for . . . in fact, this is about the time she'd go down for the night, so she shouldn't wake up to feed until long after we're home. But just in case, we'll be around the corner."

Hanna nodded, and picked up one of Anna's little onesies from a stack on the couch. "Don't worry," she said, straightening the pile again. "Even if she does wake up, I'm sure the biggest problem will be getting this one"—she pointed to Will—"to stop making googly faces at her."

Max put on his coat and helped me with mine. "No boys in the house, kids," he said. "No rated-R movies and we've left pizza money on the counter."

Will rolled his eyes and pushed us out the door. "I told you, it'll be fine," he said, waving to us from the doorway. "I outweigh her thirteen-to-one. Thirteen-to-one! What could possibly go wrong?"

There would be no fancy restaurant or sentimental bottles of wine. Instead, we stopped at a little diner a few doors down and sat at the first open table we found.

There was a sense of urgency in the air, a sense that a clock was ticking somewhere and there was zero way we'd make it through this night, maybe not even this dinner, without Will or Hanna calling with some sort of real or imagined emergency.

"You think they're going to be okay?" I asked Max, folding and refolding the paper napkin in front of me.

His eyes met mine from behind a laminated menu and he shrugged. "Of course they will. Annabel's disposition is matched only by her mother's. I can't imagine her giving anyone a problem."

I laughed. "It's possible you might be wrong on both counts, Mr. Stella."

The waiter stopped at our table and we each ordered, although I wasn't really sure why. We were at a restaurant as a formality, as a normal date-type thing before I ripped off his pants.

Which I wanted to do right now.

Our food arrived, and it took only fifteen minutes more before Max's phone buzzed on the table and he picked it up, smiling before turning the screen toward me.

"Look at him," he said. It was a photo of Will holding

Anna, his expression so proud you'd think he'd just split the atom, not changed a diaper. He was giving the camera a thumbs-up.

A very white thumbs-up, to be more accurate.

He did it! Hanna had typed.

"Is that . . ." I started to ask, squinting as I leaned in, trying to get a better look. "Is that baby powder?"

"I believe it is," Max said, looking for himself. Will looked like a powdered donut had exploded all over him. It was in his hair and eyebrows, smeared across his cheeks and covering both hands, the one supporting the baby and the one he held in front of the camera.

"He's going to have a good time cleaning that up," I said, shaking my head before finishing off my burger.

"It's good for him," Max said, replying to Hanna before setting his phone down.

"You think Will and Hanna are ready for babies?"

"I think Will would be ready for just about anything Hanna wanted. Christ, she could suggest he join a knitting group and he'd ask her what color yarn was best suited for his skin tone. Bloody brilliant watching that one so whipped. Something tells me tonight is just what they needed."

"So it's possible we might actually get a few more hours?"

Max wiped his mouth and tossed his napkin to his plate. "Don't want to jinx us, but yeah."

It had been ten minutes since Will's last text—far longer

than with George—and I got an idea. Everything was fine at home and I was *not* about to waste a golden opportunity like this one.

"What exactly is it you're doing over there, Petal?" Max said, motioning to my phone.

"Oh, just looking for something."

"Something?"

"Mm-hmm."

"Care to elaborate?"

Instead I flipped my phone so he could see the screen, and knew the exact moment he understood. "Things are going so well at home, and we'd be idiots to waste it so . . . I'm booking us a room where you can be as loud as you want and not have to keep one ear focused on a baby monitor. If you're interested, that is," I added, giving him a cheeky grin.

"Interested? I will pay everyone's bill in this bloody diner if it gets us out of here more quickly," he said, and made a hand signal at the waiter for our check. "Have I mentioned that I love you?"

"Once or twice," I said, smiling widely as the waiter set the bill on our table. I continued scrolling through the listings, and stopped when I found what I was looking for.

"So we're people who check in to hotels by the hour now?" Max joked, standing to take our bill to the register. He scratched his jaw. "I am surprisingly comfortable with this."

It was impossible not to feel like we were up to something as we checked in to a swank little hotel down the block. We had no luggage, had made the reservation less than fifteen minutes ago, and I'm sure the way I kept looking at Max—like I might throw him down on the counter at any minute—might have suggested we were up to something a bit less wholesome than a nap.

Not to mention that the New York State driver's license Max showed as proof of ID had a mailing address located less than ten minutes away. Whatever. I was going to fuck my husband; they could think whatever they want.

"If possible we'd like a room in the most empty part of the hotel," Max said. "We plan on being loud."

The clerk looked down at Max's ID and blinked back up at him again, bored, before rolling his eyes and moving to swipe our card.

Inside the elevator, Max pressed me against the far wall, pushing his hand into my hair. "Tell me what you want, sweet Sara," he said, running his nose along my jaw. "This is your night, and I want to do every filthy thing in that devious little mind of yours."

"I want you," I said. "Over me, behind me."

He hummed against my skin, and I felt every bit of anxiety melt away. He wasn't overthinking. He wasn't treating me like something he had to handle with kid gloves.

"And?" he said.

I tilted my head, looked up to see our reflections in the

mirrored ceiling of the elevator. The sight of our bodies together—even clothed—sent a shiver down my spine.

"I want your face between my legs," I told him. "I want you wild."

He exhaled, and made the tiniest, neediest sound. "You know I love how you taste. Would I lick you, Petal?"

Jesus. "Yes."

"Would I be greedy and suck, get my face covered in you? Or do you want me to take my time?"

"All of it. Rough at first and then again, slower. Savoring," I said, though who knew how much time we would actually get. I watched as Max pushed open the collar of my shirt to reveal the top swell of my breasts. I could easily imagine what we would look like from that angle: me naked on my back, legs spread shamelessly open with Max between them. I would see the flex of muscle as he devoured me, my fingers in his beautiful hair as I pulled and held him where I wanted. The flex of my toes as my orgasm moved up my body and out. As I screamed.

The elevator stopped and Max reached for my hand, practically tugging me down the hall and toward our room. "All of it," he said, slotting the key into the door. "I'll give you fucking all of it." The light glowed green as the lock clicked, and he pushed it open. Inside, it was my turn to push Max against the wall. I stood on my toes to reach his mouth, pressing my lips to his and not wasting any time as I rid us of our coats, opened his belt, and began pulling his shirt from the waist of his pants. "I want to take pictures of you," I said, and he pulled away just long enough to meet my eyes.

"Of me?"

I nodded and leaned in to suck on his bottom lip. "Of what you look like while you lick my . . . pussy."

Max groaned and let his head fall back against the door. "You have no idea what it does to hear you talk like that." I wondered if maybe this would help. If what Chloe had said was true, maybe it would be easier for him to let go if I used *him* first.

I trailed a hand over his navel and down to where he was hard and straining against the material of his pants. I gripped the shape of him, rubbing my thumb where I felt the head of his cock. "Oh, I think I have an idea of what it does to you."

Max began walking us backward, stopping just at the side of the bed. He pulled his phone from his pocket and pressed it into my hand. "Let's pray that this stays quiet, and that it's because Will has found his maternal instinct, and not because our child has suddenly learned that everyone will do precisely what she wants, and has enslaved them both."

I laughed, and set it on the bedside table.

"So what will you do with those pictures, sweet Petal?" he said, opening the buttons on my shirt one by one, and letting it slip from my shoulders.

"Look at them. Remember."

"When? At work?" he asked, and unfastened my bra,

pulling the straps down my arms, and absently tossing it into a chair against the wall. "Maybe you'll be in a meeting, everyone talking around you while you look down at your phone. They'll think you're looking at your calendar, maybe reading through an email. They'd never guess you're looking at photos of me with my face between your legs. Of your clit pressed against my tongue."

"Oh God," I said, his words mirroring *exactly* what I imagined doing. Max's eyes moved over my face, down my neck and lower. My breasts tingled, my nipples hardening with the weight of his gaze on me. My skin felt too hot, the rest of my clothes constricting.

"Would that get you wet, Petal?"

I nodded, stripping Max of his shirt first, and then his pants, finding the head of his cock visible just above the waistband of his boxers. He was so hard, the tip already wet in the setting sunlight. I licked my lips, almost able to feel the weight of him in my mouth, hard and smooth against my tongue.

"Take the rest off," Max instructed, before he reached for the bedding, pulling it down the mattress to reveal crisp, white sheets. The pile of carefully stacked pillows fell to the side and he reached for one, setting it in the middle of the bed.

I slipped out of my skirt and panties just in time for him to turn back to me and nod his approval. "Right here," he said then, motioning to the pillow. "Want that pretty little cunt up where I can get to it."

Even now, after the club and marriage and a baby and all we'd done together, I felt my cheeks heat as I did what he asked and climbed on the bed, careful to keep the pillow directly under my hips. It propped me up and I felt open and exposed, my thighs spread and the air cool against my skin. I knew that if I touched myself I'd be slick and swollen, my clit sensitive to even the smallest touch.

I kept my eyes trained on him as he stepped out of his boxers and climbed up on the bed, on his slow advance toward me. I reached out for him, wanting to feel him inside me and—

His phone vibrated on the table. *Fuck.*

I reached for it blindly, unable to look away from him and his perfect cock, the way it jutted out between us. I knocked over the alarm clock and what I assumed to be the room service menu, before I finally found what I was looking for, and held it out to him.

"Sara," Max said, and I had to tear my attention away from his body.

"Yeah?"

"The phone? You read it, yeah?" he said, and placed a hand on my knee, letting his palm smooth down my skin until it rested between my legs. "I'm a bit busy here, and unless the apartment is on fire or there's something wrong with our baby, I don't want to see a text from *anyone* right now. Just reply."

"Reply while you . . . ?" I trailed off, and he nodded.

My throat felt dry and I had to focus on what I was doing, rather than the way Max ground the heel of his hand against my clit.

"It's Will," I said, blinking down to the message. It was a close-up of Anna's face, her nose scrunched up, and her lower lip turned down into a pout. The edge of a yellow polka-dot blanket curled up near her cheek, so I assumed she was still in her crib, asleep.

What is this face? the text said.

Has she been crying? I asked, momentarily distracted from Max's fingers slipping over me.

No. Just noises. Like a puppy or something? She's ok, was just curious.

Sometimes she fusses a little while she sleeps, I typed, and had to stop and regroup when I felt Max's fingers replaced by puffs of warm breath. She usually settles herself back down! I think you're good!

That might have been a bit more enthusiastic than the situation warranted.

I waited, but when it didn't look like Will was going to respond again, I dropped the phone to the bed and groaned, throwing my head back. "Oh my God," I said, tucking my hands into Max's hair.

"Yeah?" he murmured, and licked along me in long, slow strokes.

"*Fuck yes.*"

"Taste so fucking good, Petal," he said, circling his

tongue around my clit and murmuring the words right against me.

I opened my legs wider and held him there, rocking my hips up to meet his mouth until I was practically fucking his face. "More, Max," I said, looking down at him. "And fingers?"

Max did as I asked, and I felt as he slipped first one finger inside of me, and then a second. "The camera, Petal," he said, and I remembered the phone sitting on the mattress next to me. Max pressed his mouth to me again, lips wrapped around my clit as he sucked and sucked, even humming. My hands shook as I aimed the camera at him, touching the screen with trembling fingers as I took photo after photo.

Max made a little noise each time the camera clicked, and the thought that this was what was getting him off—that I would look at these later and think of him and this and his sounds—made it hard not to flip him over and fuck him right then.

With two fingers pumping in and out of me, he turned his head, sucking and pressing kisses into the pale skin of my thigh, and me nearly screaming as the single day's growth of beard brushed against my clit. It was so much. He looked up at me, eyes meeting mine as his tongue peeked out, and I moved to focus the camera again, to capture that moment, when another text flashed across the screen.

How do you heat the milk? it read. Hanna says we

do it under water but I told her we can do it in the microwave provided we use a digital thermometer and warm it to body temperature or 98.7 degrees. WHO'S RIGHT SARA

It took me three attempts to finally type out a simple LISTEN TO HANNA before I threw the phone down and had to bite my forearm to keep from screaming.

Max had pulled away a bit, concerned that something might be wrong, but I waved him off.

"It's fine it's fine," I said, embarrassingly breathless. "Don'tstopohgodplease. Keep," I started, but had to lick my lips, and suck in another desperate lungful of air. "Keepgoingplease please please. I'm so close."

Max redoubled his efforts, licking and sucking my clit, and somewhere, through the fog of what was happening, I heard him groan, heard the sound of his hand working over his cock.

"Oh God . . . are you?" I started, attempting to push myself up and look, but the phone went off again.

I groaned in defeat, so close I could cry.

She's not taking it, it said. Are we sure she needs to eat this much? There's no way an actual human could eat this much. When you figure in her size in comparison to how many ounces of fluid she consumes . . .

"What the fuck does he want now?" Max said, and pushed himself up on his hands.

"Anna won't eat for him," I started, and Max let his

cheek fall to my hip. "Max, I'm beginning to think this isn't going to work. I'm never going to have an orgasm and you're going to have to adjust to a life of blue balls."

"Fuck that," he said. "Give me five more minutes, I can do it, I swear."

But it was no use. I wanted him—*God, did I want him*—but now all I could think about was my tiny baby crying at home, hungry.

We both lay there for a moment, trying to calm our breaths and . . . other things, before we got up.

"We'll get the hang of this, Petal," Max said, climbing up my body so he could kiss my forehead. "We've got all the time in the world."

I went to reply to Will, to tell him we were on our way home, but instead stared in horror at my screen. Somehow, while juggling the camera and texts . . . *holy shit, I'd texted Will a picture of Max's head between my legs.*

"Oh . . . oh, my God," I groaned, handing Max my phone so he could see what I'd done. "I should not be in charge of the camera anymore."

I rolled into the pillow with another groan as Max read Will's reply and burst out laughing: Okay . . . that was unexpected but message received. Take your time. We'll figure out the milk thing.

Five

SARA

I'd seen photos of Niall Stella, so of course I was prepared for the resemblance between my brother-in-law and my husband—same lighter brown hair, same warm brown eyes, *way* too pretty to be fair—but what I wasn't prepared for was the impact of having not one, but two Stella men standing in the doorway of our apartment.

Niall let a black leather laptop bag slip from his shoulder, and straightened to his full height, before smiling widely at his brother.

He was just as tall as Max, but a bit more on the slender side. Years of rugby had left Max with broader shoulders and arms and legs defined by ropes of thick muscle. Niall was definitely built, but leaner, the type of build with wide shoulders and narrow hips. A body designed to wear a suit.

From the way he walked into the apartment, it was

clear he was comfortable in his own skin, but he was quieter, missing that boisterous quality that seemed to seep into a room whenever Max entered it. In its place was a gentle confidence and a touch of vulnerability that made me want to push Max out of the way and hug Niall myself.

Niall had been unable to come to the States for our small, last-minute wedding ceremony—he'd been in the middle of a divorce, a new job—but had promised to come as soon as he was able. I knew he and Max, being only ten months apart, were the closest of the siblings, and Max had been more excited for this visit than he'd wanted to let on.

Max loved Will and Bennett—and there wasn't a situation in which I could imagine him not doing whatever it took to help out his boys—but it had nothing on the embrace he gave his younger brother. The two men wrapped their arms around each other in an all-encompassing hug, and maybe it was the hormones talking but it's possible the closed eyes and small smile on each of their faces might have left me a bit teary. Maybe.

Max whispered something in Niall's ear I couldn't make out, before he clapped him on the back and pulled him inside. It was clear that Max had been even more worried about his brother than he realized.

"It's been too long," Max said, reaching for Niall's bag before closing the door.

"Absolutely," Niall said, and oh. *Two* British men under my roof. I didn't stand a chance.

I stepped out of the hallway and into the living room, and offered Niall a small wave when I caught his eye.

"And you must be the lovely Sara," he said, crossing the room to place a kiss on my cheek. "So lovely to finally meet you."

Niall was a great hugger, bending at the knees and wrapping his arms completely around me. When he pulled back to meet my eyes, I almost swooned.

"I can see what has him so smitten," Niall said.

"Truer words were never spoken," Max said.

"I may need the two of you to cut down on the cute for a bit," I said. "I'm not sure I can handle it."

"We'll do our best, Petal," Max said with a wink, and led Niall to the living room. "You look bloody fantastic. Divorce suits you."

Max had explained the circumstances behind Niall and Portia's divorce, that they'd married when they were fresh out of high school, and been with only each other up until the previous summer, when they both decided it wasn't working anymore. Max also told me that "not working anymore" was code for *Portia was a beast.*

If Max's comment bothered Niall at all, he didn't show it. Instead, he sank back against the sofa and exhaled in what looked like his first real breath in a very long time.

"You know I would never speak poorly of Portia," Niall

said, shaking his head with a smile, "but yes. I feel better than I have in years."

A small sound emanated from the baby monitor on the end table, and I stood, explaining that I'd go get the baby up from her nap.

I could hear the men talking while I changed Anna's diaper, hear the clink of their beer bottles and laughter, and I smiled down at my daughter.

"Ready to go meet your uncle?" I whispered, and she cooed, smiling up at me and kicking her little sock-covered feet. I gathered her up and we made our way into the living room, and both men stopped. Max looked like the proudest daddy in the world, but Niall looked completely in awe.

"She's breathtaking," Niall said, setting his bottle on the table and standing to meet me. "She's absolutely bloody gorgeous, Sara. Well done."

"She's a beauty, yeah?" Max crossed the room to take her from me, kissing me on the forehead before sitting next to his brother.

"Mum must be over the moon," Niall said, running a finger along the edge of the blanket.

"You've no idea," Max said. "I'll be at her flat not five minutes before she's nicked her from me."

My heart swelled as I watched them together, and I took a few steps back and into the kitchen, leaving them alone while they caught up.

Tired from a long day of travel, Niall excused himself for the night around the same time I tucked Annabel in her crib.

With the apartment blissfully silent, I shut off lights and made a final check of the front door before finding Max in our room, folding tiny pink onesies and socks, and placing them in a basket on the bed. I lay down next to him and watched.

"You're pretty sexy when you're domestic," I told him, running a hand up the back of his thigh.

"If you think this is hot, you should see me change a diaper."

"I have, actually; why do you think I married you? That and your accent. Oh and your giant penis."

"Too right," he said, and bent to kiss me. "And I married you because you're lovely and smart and sexy as hell. Not to mention the fact that you can take on the world."

"Taking on the world," I said, folding a pair of socks. "Guess I'll be going back to that soon enough."

Max set the basket aside and kneeled on the floor in front of me. "Are you not ready, Petal?"

I picked up one of Anna's little T-shirts, one that fit her only weeks ago and was now ready to be packed away. I barely remembered her in that shirt, and she had *just* outgrown it. What in the world would I miss when I was gone all day? And yet . . .

"I am," I said honestly. "I'm just having a hard time shutting out that guilty voice over *wanting* to go back to work."

"Why on earth would you want to silence it? Let yourself feel all the things, Sara. Then take a step back and realize that you can do whatever you bloody want. You can take over the world *and* still be the world's greatest mother and wife. Annabel will grow up seeing you do all the things and know that she can do all things, too, if she chooses."

Max got up and sat next to me on the bed.

"And I've been thinking. I know you want to go back to the club, and I want you to know that I want that, too. I was thinking over something we talked about the other day, how there was a time when it felt like Annabel never slept. But slowly, we got through it?"

I nodded.

"Maybe that will be our new rule. We figure it out as we go."

"You know, I was thinking the same thing. I've been so set on proving that I'm the same—that we are—but we're not, are we? And we don't have to be. I love this new life and I love the new you, just as much as the old one. Maybe even more."

Max leaned in and tilted my chin up to meet him before pressing a slow, lingering kiss to my lips. "I like the sound of that," he said. "So you'll go back to work, and we continue to do this." He kissed each of my cheeks and then motioned between us. "Doing what works best for *us*. I'm actually looking forward to having her with me more at the office, and Mum—not to mention Will—will be thrilled."

I pulled Max to lie next to me, and fit my leg between his thighs. "You know, everyone's asleep."

"You think you could be quiet with what I'd do to you? I'm insulted," he said, smiling against my mouth.

"I don't know. But I'd certainly be willing to try. Maybe you could gag me?"

Max's eyes widened before he started unbuttoning the top of my dress. "I think we can work something out. In fact—"

As if on cue, Annabel picked that exact moment to start wailing.

"Let's give her a minute. She might just fall back to sleep." I told him, tucking my face into his neck. He smelled so good, like the Max I had always known, but a little like Anna, too. He was getting *so* laid.

Two minutes of crying went by, and I had just extricated myself from Max's arms to go pick her up, when the apartment fell silent.

We looked at each other, before both of us turned our attention down the hall. "What is that?" Max asked.

I listened, unable to make out the soft humming I could

hear from the living room. We both stood and quickly dressed, before we began tiptoeing down the hall.

We turned the corner and Max stopped, quickly enough that I ran into his back. "What is it?" I whispered.

Max moved over the tiniest bit, and there was Niall: tie off and top of his shirt unbuttoned, shoeless and walking back and forth, talking softly to a bright-eyed Annabel.

"Well I'll be damned," Max said. "Didn't take long for her to fall in love with him. Not that I'm surprised, mind you."

"That's it, baby girl," he murmured, kissing her softly on one of her puffy cheeks.

Anna continued to look up at him in awe, and Max and I turned to look at each other.

"Niall's a natural," I whispered to Max.

He looked back at his brother, before turning back to me. "Are you thinking what I'm thinking?"

Six

MAX

I stared at my brother the next morning as he took a bite of toast and scanned the business section, oblivious to my inspection. It had been too long since our last visit—longer than we'd ever been apart. Marriages beginning and ending, careers growing, babies born, family obligations, and a myriad of other obstacles had kept me from England and him from the States. Though I was only ten months older than him, seeing him here brought back the older-brother protectiveness his calm stoicism had always triggered in me.

Because he rarely said otherwise, I needed to make sure he really was doing all right.

He looked thinner, but fitter, too. I meant it when I said divorce suited him. Instead of seeming beat down by the taxing drag of the proceedings, it seemed as if a literal weight had been removed from his shoulders. His face was less shadowed, mouth less drawn. He smiled easily again.

Of all my siblings, Niall and I were the most similar physically but dissimilar mentally. We were both tall, had tended toward athletic builds, and had our father's lighter brown hair. But whereas it had taken me years to get my head on straight about school and birds and the bleeding enormous what-to-do-with-my-life decisions, Niall was born thinking like a little engineer: logical, calm, meticulous. I'd worked my way through most of Manhattan's single women; he'd married the first girl he kissed. I had barely found a single job I loved until I met Will and we started the firm together; Niall had excelled in civil engineering so early he'd been the second in command at the London Underground when he was only twenty-eight before being wooed away to a private firm. I spoke freely, shared too readily, loved perhaps too openly. Niall considered every word before he let it out, held his private truths close to his chest, and had never been with a woman who let him love openly at all.

"How's the ex-monster?" I asked.

"Portia's mostly off doing whatever it is she does," he told me, letting out a quiet laugh. "I get the occasional note about needing to fix this or that at the flat."

I felt the familiar protective heat rise in my chest. "She can hire out for that. Lord knows she has enough of her own money, as well as yours."

"She can, indeed," he agreed with the genuine smile of a man finally liberated.

I hated what Portia had done to him. She'd started with

a shy, sweet, and devoted teenage Niall and left us with a deeply emotionally reserved version of the same man. I didn't mind his reserve; I didn't even mind his new emotional discipline. I missed the lad with the easy dimpled smile and enormous, curious eyes.

But fuck it. He was here in my flat, finally coming back to life.

"You should have fucked Teena Smith at Robbie's party when I told you to," I said to him.

He barely missed a beat: "*Oi*, this again. I was already with—"

"Oh, fuck Portia. Teena would have bounced on your knob for days."

He laughed, scratching his jaw. "A bit too eager, though, yeah?"

"Eager with a cocksucking mouth and great tits."

"Great tits," he agreed ruefully. "Bloody great tits."

"Who had great tits?" Sara asked, walking into the kitchen to grab her coffee.

"Teena," Niall and I answered in unison.

"The one I should have shagged," Niall explained further.

"And it's unfortunate he didn't," I explained. "Portia would have married that insufferable arse Richard, and Niall would have been a sex god in uni instead of saddled with a wife and mortgage."

He hummed, blowing over the surface of his hot tea as his eyes returned to the paper. "Maybe."

Sara looked at us with a sweetly quizzical grin before leaving again.

"So." I brought my coffee to my lips.

He smiled without looking up. "Hmm?"

"Good to have you visit."

My brother nodded, sipping his tea. "Been too long."

"Everything good across the pond?"

Shrugging, he said, "Same, I suppose? There's a chance I'll be back in a few weeks' time for a summit here."

"Yeah?" I said, a little more eagerly than I'd intended.

He nodded. "I'll be around a bit more, you see. So you might as well just bring up whatever it is you're working up to."

"Oh, you mean the thing about how you're watching the child tonight while I take my woman out for some fun?"

He brought his toast to his mouth and smiled around it, "Yes, that thing."

"We'll be out late," I warned.

"I certainly hope so." He maintained eye contact, eyes wry and knowing as he chewed, swallowed.

"I'm not going to tell you what we're doing, if that's what you think."

He laughed, shaking his head as he poured some more tea. "Well, until you said that, I assumed it was just dinner. Now I think maybe I'd rather not know."

Sara brought Anna out into the kitchen, making her way over to me, but Niall wiped his mouth and his hands with a napkin before he reached for the baby. "Come here, love. Guess who gets to watch you tonight?"

Sara folded the baby in his arms and turned to the fridge, pulling out a bottle of milk. "Are you sure?"

He nodded. "Might kick you out myself."

She smiled at him gratefully. "Well, I'm leaving around six, but there's plenty of bottles in here for the rest of the night," she said, looking at him over her shoulder. "We use this bottle warmer. See?" She put the bottle in, pushed the button, and we all watched as it began to steam, and then beeped when it was done. "Easy."

"We'll manage fine," he said, taking the bottle and expertly shaking it to warm the milk evenly as he looked down at Anna again. "Won't we, princess?"

Watching him like this, I realized how much more experience he had with babies than I did: between our eight siblings there were seventeen nieces and nephews, and Niall was the favorite uncle to them all.

Sara put her hand on his shoulder. "Thanks for doing this."

He waved her off, making one of his stiff, dismissive grunts.

"That's awkward Brit for 'you're welcome,'" I said, laughing as I waited for Anna to push the bottle away and cry for Sara.

Niall gazed down at her as he offered her the milk. "That's a girl. Who's a good baby?" He bent and kissed her forehead. "Ah, but she's a hungry one, isn't she?"

I gaped at him, at her tiny hand clutching his thumb as she drank happily.

Bloody hell.

If my daughter had one superpower it would be the ability to locate her mum from several rooms away. If Sara were anywhere in the house, Anna wouldn't dare take a bottle from me.

I scowled at Niall. "You must smell like a woman."

"Piss off," he said to me, still using his baby-soothing voice. "Why is your daddy such a wanker, hmm? I've got a hundred nieces and nephews and he expects I can't give this tiny miss a bottle?"

Laughing, I stood and cleared our dishes.

"Baby girl knows which uncle's gonna spoil her rotten," Niall whispered just loud enough for me to hear. "Who wants a pony? Is it you? You do? I'll make sure you get a pony."

I groaned, smacking the back of his head as I walked past him to go find Sara.

"You're welcome, wanker," he sang sweetly.

༺

I FOUND SARA IN the bathroom, putting on the pair of diamond earrings her father sent after Anna was born.

Bending to kiss her neck, I said, "I'll have Scott come for us here at eight—"

"No." She turned to face me, running her hands up my dress shirt and straightening my collar. "Don't."

I blinked, tilting my head as my stomach dropped. Had she changed her mind? "You don't want to go?"

Her smile was a sweet reassurance. "Of course I do. But I want to meet there. Scott can bring me. You come separately."

She wanted to leave for the club separately? "But we've always gone together."

"I don't want to drag anything behind us when we leave. If he picks us both up here, we'll fuss over the details of leaving Anna, we'll talk about her in the car. I think I'm going to take her out and do some back-to-work shopping then head to your mom's. I'll coordinate with Niall. Scott can get me there and I'll see you at Johnny's. We can just be *us* tonight."

"You sure?"

She pulled her lip between her teeth and smiled around it before whispering, "Yeah, I'm sure."

Innocence, anticipation, lust, and something sweeter than pure sugar. It was everything I loved about Sara distilled into a single expression.

"Right then. I'll meet you there at nine."

I LEFT FOR WORK, expecting to see Sara at lunch, or even get a call from her as I usually did during the day, but knowing I might not. I suspected Sara might want a little distance today to help put her in the right mind-set, and I was right. A text came just as the office was clearing out, to let me know Niall was picking Annabel up at Mum's flat and she would meet me at the club, as planned.

The distance was odd, but also thrilling.

I went home, showered and dressed, and walked through the rooms of my empty flat. Niall had rung to say he'd be back with the baby shortly, and I had to admit that I agreed with Sara, it would be better if I left before they got here. Annabel was in excellent hands, and Max and Sara as parents could be put on hold for a few hours.

There was nothing left to do; it was time to meet my wife.

My phone buzzed on my way out, a text from Johnny: Use the front door.

We always came in through the back hallway and directly into Room Six. Having performed dozens of times at the club, Sara and I were recognizable to nearly everyone who would be there on a Wednesday night. Johnny wanted her to walk in, right in the middle of all of that?

My protective instinct flared.

Did Sara request this? I replied.

Shut up. In a fucking meeting.

This was as good as a yes; if it was for any other reason he would have said so.

Laughing, I replied in eight separate messages:
It's
A
Shame
About
Your
Tiny
Shriveled
Dick

ONCE I CONFIRMED WITH our driver Scott that he was picking Sara up at my mother's flat, I called for a cab to get me over to the club, Red Moon. I'd put on something simple, not knowing how Johnny would have the room set up for our return to the club. I wore black trousers and a simple pressed gray check button-down shirt. It had been so long since we came in through the secretive front entrance that I was actually nervous—wanting to make sure I remembered how to get down there: with a key, down several flights to the receptionist. Except standing at the desk waiting my arrival wasn't Lisbeth, but a stunning redhead who circled the desk, hand outstretched.

"I'm Trin," she said, smiling in welcome. "You must be Mr. Stella."

BEAUTIFUL BELOVED

I fucked my wife for everyone to see in this club. It seemed a little odd to be so formal. "Max, please."

"Lovely to meet you." She gestured to the heavy steel door that would lead into the club itself. "Mr. French is very much looking forward to having you and Mrs. Stella back in the rotation."

I smiled, arching a brow. "The pony play and multiple ménage scenarios are growing a little tired?"

She laughed, shaking her head. "I think the regulars like your story," she said. "It's sweet. It's different from everything else we get in here."

And of course it was. What other married couple would let their most intimate moments play out in such stark display for complete strangers? Who else would invite the world into their sex life?

But being back here, even in this unfamiliar anteroom to the main event, felt deliciously surreal. I could smell the mix of wood polish and leather emanating from the other room. I could hear the faint beat of music pounding through the enormous door. It was a sensory trigger for me, being here, knowing how Sara would get off on being watched, and how I would get off on watching her bloom. It never ceased to amaze me that her greatest turn-on was exhibition, given that in our everyday life she was beautiful but unassuming, brilliant but endlessly humble.

"How's the baby?" Trin asked, pulling my attention away from the door and back to her face.

"She's brilliant, yeah," I said, feeling my grin split my face. "Home with my brother."

Her eyebrows rose wickedly. "You have a brother?"

"I do," I said through a laugh. "He's tall, a genius, and has enough repressed sexual energy to power this club. I should give you his number."

Trin tilted her head before finding a card in the top drawer of her desk with her name and phone number. "Give him this." She turned and gestured that I lead us to the door. "Mrs. Stella is inside. I don't want to keep you."

Through the door, the club opened into a large main room, dimly lit with wall sconces and lined with a lavish, intricate wallpaper of subtle stripes and swirls. Velvet curtains hung beside a number of small alcoves surrounding low tables, making the entire room feel both lavish and faintly medieval. A small bar stood in the corner, where I remembered, but the design of the room had been modified so that the stage was directly in the center, rather than jutting into the floor from one far end of the expansive space.

Sara was tucked into an alcove in the middle of one long wall, sipping a cocktail and looking surprisingly comfortable all on her own here. She watched the show— a woman stripping to a slow beat while a man behind her was tied naked to a chair.

It was surreal how quickly my brain switched from the daily reality of diapers and investors, bottles and contracts, to the present reality of a private—and rather illegal—space where only the most well-connected and wealthy clients came to indulge their darkest voyeuristic fantasies. It didn't seem odd that the woman performing was stripped down to a long string of pearls hanging heavily between her small breasts, or that the man had begun quietly begging for pleasure. All around us, people sipped drinks and talked in low voices or simply sat and watched the main show, waiting for the individual rooms to open for the audience.

There were six other rooms in this club, connected to the main room by a long hallway. The setup was simple: each room had a different scene to watch, with tables outside a window looking in. Clients could have drinks while enjoying a perfect view of some of the darkest, sweetest, and filthiest fantasies come to life.

Some of the performers in the club were regulars—experienced Doms, Broadway performers with exhibitionist leanings earning some good money on the side, or dancers who were willing to try anything—and some were vague acquaintances of Johnny who had begged him for the opportunity to perform at the prestigious club. Sara and I were the only friends of his granted a consistent time slot: Wednesday nights were ours in Room Six for as long as we wanted.

Though we never took money—unlike a few others who "performed" at the club—Wednesday night in Room Six grew to be one of the most popular acts in the place, and quite a profitable show for Johnny. The only reason Sara and I knew this, however, was that he told us. We never saw a single face in our audience; other than our first night and until tonight, we'd only ever come into the club through the back entrance.

And just on my short walk from the front door to the table, I could feel the rustle of movement, the way people sat up straight in realization. I could feel the subtle gestures, the quiet whisper of *They're back*.

Had Sara felt it, too?

Had she liked it? I felt a shiver climb up my spine, felt my heart begin to thunder at the idea that she was sitting here, thinking of how many times these people had watched me fuck her. Thinking of her growing wet at just the *idea* of it all.

Sara looked up when Trin led me over to her, and stood, making my blood come to a thudding stop in my veins.

She wore a short black dress, simple but with a beading detail that gave just a hint of sparkle. It would look amazing under the lights, I realized, then smiled when I noted that it would look even better *off*, lying in a pool on the floor. Her eyes were lined with a soft brown, her lips an edible red. There was nothing particularly special about how she had put herself together tonight, but the heat in her eyes—the devilish fire, the flirtatious tilt of her mouth, the way she looked at my face for only a beat before ogling my body—set my skin into a heated flush.

Bending, I kissed her jaw. "Hello, Petal." I inhaled the sweetness of her skin, dragging my lips to her ear. "You look fucking *beautiful*."

"Hey, Stranger." She sat, glancing at the space on the bench beside her as if to say that I was meant to be immediately beside her, and not across the table. There were strict rules at the club: two-drink maximum, no touching between clients, everyone is there by choice and any evidence to the contrary results in the fist of God—aka Johnny—coming down.

I knew I wasn't supposed to touch Sara out here on the main floor, but did the rules really apply to us, when it was clear that we were part of the show? More people were watching us at our tiny table than were watching the naked woman deep-throating the man bound to the chair in the middle of the room.

Sitting beside, her, I leaned close, sucking at her neck.

"Max," she warned.

"They're watching," I told her. "You think they want to see me come in here and follow the rules?" I kissed my way to her mouth, parting her lips with mine and sucking deeply on her tongue before whispering, "I haven't seen you all day. I'm going to greet you the way I bloody well feel I should. Fuck Johnny and his rules."

And proving that I was right, no one appeared at the side of our table asking us to leave.

No one signaled a warning to me across the room.

Instead, it felt like the entire room held its breath, watching.

"How long have you been here?" I asked.

She shrugged, tucking her long hair behind her ear. That was another thing that had changed over the past year. Her hair had grown out, curves had bloomed. "About ten minutes before you."

I studied her face—the pink flush to her cheeks, the quick intake of breaths, the way her gaze could barely stray from my mouth. "Did you feel them watching you?"

She nodded.

"Was it weird?"

She shook her head slowly before whispering, "No."

I slid my hand under the table, up her bare thighs to the soft lace of her underwear beneath. I could feel the heat through, warming my fingers. "Did it make you wet?"

She watched my mouth. "Yeah."

"What do you think they remember the most?" I rubbed my fingers over her clit beneath the lace, kissed her cheek, and then moved to her lips, kissing her once at the fullest part of her perfect fucking mouth.

"Maybe the time I tied you up," she said, taking my face in her hands so she could tilt my head and scrape her teeth over my jaw. "Or maybe the first time we . . ." She trailed off, smiling knowingly.

I nodded. The first time we'd had anal sex, we'd had it here. Somehow it felt safer, slower. Her hunger, her surprise, her pleasure had been so raw. I was sure as soon as she said it that if anyone here tonight had seen it, they would never forget the soft curved shape of her mouth when she felt me fully inside her, and when she came harder than I think she ever had before.

The attention in the room ebbed and returned, ricocheting between the main act and us. We were the quieter option; we had *always* been the quiet act. What we offered wasn't hard kink, it was simply *us*—a relationship that deepened, trust that intensified, sexual exploration that matured. What we received in return was a safe place to try it all. Their focus was a paradoxical sort of respect: they watched nearly every move we made but they loved it. They were invested.

We didn't normally drink much before a show, but since this particular occasion seemed to be about breaking all the rules—arriving separately, entering through the front door, and touching each other on the main floor—I waved the waitress over with a subtle lift of my hand. She brought me a vodka gimlet, and Sara ordered a club soda with lime.

I was so excited for what would follow that my hand

nearly trembled as I lifted the glass to my mouth, which was all the more reason to do this. I needed to be calm, to settle into the atmosphere before we walked back to our room. We sipped our drinks as we watched the others around us, and wordlessly agreed to save the real show for Room Six.

A tall woman in a flowing pink negligee, nothing but glittering pink pasties visible beneath, stepped to our table, signaling that it was time.

I followed Sara as she stood, and sensed the way the room grew still. As we headed toward the hallway, I could hear the quiet shuffle of chairs pushed back from tables, of footsteps following at a respectable distance.

"You ready for this?" I asked her.

I could hear her smile: "Yeah."

My heart seemed intent on hammering its way up my throat. We passed the scenes in the other rooms to our left.

An orgy of men.

An older woman masturbating a man who had such a young face, he may have turned legal only today.

I watched Sara walk confidently past clientele who looked up as she passed as if they knew her. I felt their eyes on my face.

To our left, a woman behind the glass was tied up and being prepared for anal penetration.

I could see the door to our room just around the slight bend and my body seemed to come to life.

I never knew what to expect as far as room décor went; some nights Johnny kept Room Six simple, with a bed and nothing more. Other nights it looked like my living room, a lavish hotel room, or, once, even a tropical bungalow.

Tonight Mr. French had gone with simple: a gleaming silver rolling cart with a decanter of scotch and some chocolates, a plush rug covering most of the smooth wood floor, and an enormous bed in the middle of the room. Soft plum-colored sheets covered the mattress but it was otherwise bare.

I walked to the rolling cart, looking over my shoulder at Sara. Already the thrill of being here overwhelmed me; I needed to distract myself with an activity other than throwing her onto the mattress and defiling her.

"Do you want a drink?" I asked. I poured myself a small bit of scotch and looked up at her.

"Sure. A little of that." She nodded to the bottle in my hand. Sara rarely drank hard alcohol, but, again: breaking all the rules. She looked so in her element right now, so fucking thrilled. I could tell by the flush of her neck how much the walk down that hall had turned her on.

I poured her a small glass of whisky and she took it from me before dipping a finger in it and painting a wet line across her neck.

An invitation.

"We're starting, then?"

Her laugh was a quiet, husky thing. "We started an hour ago."

I downed my shot, took a step closer, and bent to suck her neck.

"The last time we were here, I was pregnant," she whispered, and I wondered how firm the pressure of attention through the mirrored glass felt against her back.

"You were glorious," I corrected her.

"Tell me what we did that night."

"We were lying down," I said, looking over to the far side of the room where the bed had been that time, right up against the mirrored window that let others see in where we couldn't see out. "I was curled behind you, taking you like that."

"Gently," she interjected, laughing.

I smiled into her shoulder, nipping it. "Despite your efforts, yes, gently. But I watched you come with a scream, in the mirror just as clearly as they did."

Her fingers moved up my chest and touched the bare skin beneath the collar of my shirt. "And then what happened?"

Inhaling deeply, I closed my eyes as the memory caused my heart to pound harder, squeeze faster. "Your water broke in the car on the way home."

"And then what?"

And then what.

And then we turned around, drove to the hospital in a heady fog of terror and glee, and I burst into the ER, carrying Sara in my arms and yelling for help like she'd been shot instead of simply gone into labor.

"And then Annabel Dillon Stella was born thirty hours later."

"We had a *baby*, Max." Her chin was tilted up in her badass, proud smile.

I smiled down at her, feeling my chest expand until it consumed the entire world. "Yeah we fucking did."

She ran her hand down my torso and cupped the swollen tip of my cock in her palm, pushing and slowly stroking it through my trousers. Just like that. There was no transition topic. No need to distance herself from remembering having our baby to touching me like that. No space between Sara the mum and Sara my lover.

"And here we are again," she said, stretching to kiss my throat. "Just being in this room makes me feel wild. I love it so much."

I closed my eyes and groaned. "I love *you*."

"And I love you." I felt her stretch, graze her teeth over my neck. "What do you think it's like for them to watch us tonight?"

I blinked over her shoulder and gazed at the giant mirror. "I think it's a milder version of how it feels for us to *be* here tonight."

"Like they're on this journey with us, kind of."

"Yeah," I agreed. "Did you feel them following down the hall?"

"All of them." She tilted her head back, running her hands into my hair as I bent and kissed lower, to her breastbone through her silk top. "I always knew people were watching. I just didn't know it was nearly *everyone*."

I unzipped her dress and slipped it down her shoulders inch by inch, feeling like I was seeing her new body through their eyes. Knowing they could see what I did—the fuller breasts, the return of her narrow waist. They would see her tonight without the benefit of transition—from lush and pregnant to her body now: slim, ripe, fucking wicked. She was a siren half naked in her delicate dress, her nails a soft pink, lips full and wet. Soft. Everything about her was so fucking *soft*.

I blinked away but not before glancing quickly to where I knew people were watching, knowing each and every one of them could see my sharp possessiveness and pride.

Look at her, I thought, reaching to unhook her bra. *Look at this beautiful fucking woman.*

Her breasts were firm when I cupped one, and a flush of warmth pulsed through me when I registered she hadn't pumped before she came here.

"*Jesus,* Sare."

"Own it, Stella." She tugged my shirt from my pants with a devious little smirk. "If we're going to play tonight, we're going to *play*." Sara unbuttoned my jeans and slid her hand into my boxers. "In here you don't get to pretend it doesn't make you crazy to suck on them or get your palms all wet. You don't get to pretend my body like this is for her. It's for you, too. You did it. *Own* it."

She pressed the heel of her palm into me and let out a quiet groan. I was so rigid it skirted the line of pleasure and true discomfort. *This* is what she did to me. Scooped out every thought and sensation so she could fill me up with nothing but this searing ache for her.

"They're going to watch you and wonder how it feels," she said, "whether you like it." Her voice dropped to a whisper as she ran the nail of her index finger along my collarbone: "They're going to wonder how often you fuck them."

I could barely look at her like this—rapt and sexy and self-possessed—without feeling a heavy swell of emotion in my chest. I swallowed, hands shaking as I pushed her dress down her hips. Her need was a tangible thing, growing and filling the room, and it started to consume me, too, knowing what it would feel like in the tiny slide of skin between her legs. How slick and wet she would feel on my fingers.

The fabric pooled on the floor—looking every bit as good as I'd anticipated—and I didn't bother to lower her lacy pants before I slid my hand down in them, fingers searching and finding her soaked.

"*Fuck.*"

"They're wondering why your mouth isn't on my breast," she whispered, pulling my head down until I licked at the tight pink swell, until I felt the sweetness draw across my tongue. I groaned, squeezing her with a hand that had started to feel a little greedy, more than a little wild. She slid her hands down my back. "They're wondering what it's like to play with them like this."

I sucked, groaning and turning her until she faced the mirror and could watch what they watched: me, bent at the waist to reach her breasts, licking them into a wet shine, making them grow fuller and tighter.

"I'll fuck them," I whispered.

"Yeah," she gasped.

"I'll come all over that pretty neck and then lick your pussy so deep they'll see in my face how sweet you taste."

She pushed me until I reached the mattress and sat and then straddled me, bending to seal her mouth to mine. I let out a sound between a groan and a plea for more when her tongue pushed into my mouth, tiny and sweet but commanding, hungry to feel and dominate. I loved my Sara like this, in charge and powerful, fists in my hair so she could pull my head back and get me at whatever angle she wanted. She fucking owned every cell in my body, every breath, every reflex.

I could barely move my hands from her breasts, working and kneading, loving the feel of the tightness in my hands and the wet on my palms. I swiveled her so her back faced the mirror and they could see the slide of my hands around her ribs, over her back, down to her ass.

She ground down over my cock, and then pushed me until I was lying on my back so she could peel my trousers and boxers off in a fierce, determined tug.

"Socks," I commanded quietly, and she giggled as she finished undressing me completely.

My wife gave me a look that communicated some pretty wicked intentions before she licked her way up my legs and pushed them apart to draw her tongue across my balls.

"Filthy fucking girl," I said through a laugh, closing my eyes as she drew her slick tongue up my cock. I pulled her hair into my fist and guided her as she was sloppy and wild all over me. Pushing onto an elbow, I reached to spank her tight ass with my other hand and groaned when she pushed herself deep onto my cock in response, swallowing the tip deep into her throat.

It was *too* good—too much wet and suction and pull along my length if I was going to last at all—and I pulled out and flipped Sara to her back, smiling at her surprised giggle and climbed over her ribs, pushing her tits around my cock. I was still slick from her mouth and I rocked over her, fucking with a sort of savage abandon I hadn't let myself feel in so long. I might bruise her and I could tell neither of us cared. I could come all over her neck, defile her, feel the tip of my cock hit the delicate skin of her throat and it was the kind of rough and possessive behavior, I could see from her expression, that she needed.

She'd missed seeing me like this, I knew. She'd missed seeing me obsessed and hungry to claim, seeing me overcome and wild. Did she really need to be reminded? I told her every day she was beautiful. Every night she felt my desire for her when she curled against me. But of course, here it was different: here we were more bare somehow than we were even in our bedroom, as if constantly raising the stakes of what we were willing to share with the people on the other side of the window.

We gave them a show but it was never false. It was as if it was a game where we could unveil every dark or wicked thought we had, every needy impulse, every vulnerability that needed to be given attention.

See? she said with her eyes. *You forgot how much I love to see you wild for me. You forgot this is where we play with fetish and boundaries.*

But I remembered.

And it was the *best* game. I could see the moment she felt it, too, because her lips parted in this elated smile and she laughed, sliding her fingers over me and arching her spine to press my cock harder into her skin.

I was close, could feel the ache behind my naval build and spin downward until I was wild—one hand braced beside her head while I fucked earnestly, hips pivoting faster and harder over her until the growling sound I heard was my own voice, warning her, begging her, telling her how hard I was going to come and where.

Her neck.

Her tits.

Her chin and bottom lip when she bent, wide-eyed, watching me spill out onto her.

Still gasping, I slid down her body, smearing my hand down her wet skin and resting my palm on her belly as I settled between her legs, kissing her hip, her thigh, and finally the sweetness just between her legs. Her hands found their way into my hair and pulled, hips lifting from the mattress, circling as I sucked and licked at her, knowing how to make it fast and easy, knowing how to make the hoarse cries tear from her throat when she came, and then slowed, smiling up at her eyes closed in relief, her upper lip glistening with sweat.

I rose to my knees and slid my fingers into her, watching from above as I pumped them, fucking her. I'd seen her naked in every conceivable way—spread wide beneath me like this, or showering alone, begging for more pleasure or less pain, absorbed in my touch and oblivious to my proximity—and there was something so intimate, so *safe*, about sharing this sight of her but being the only one who could ever touch her, who would ever know each of those quieter moments. No one else would ever see her give birth to our child or bend and shave her legs in the bath. No one else would ever see her sleeping, curled around a pillow in our bed or nursing our daughter at four in the morning. So the owners of each set of eyes out there watching her come apart under my touch would never, not in a million years, be able to give her what I gave her. For Sara, nothing turned her on more profoundly than my total, obliterating adoration.

Every second that I loved her—a love story for the ages condensed into not even two years—coalesced into this single fucking touch. My hand slowed, fingers carefully pulling from her as I bent and covered her body with mine, covered her lips with mine. I was nearly hard enough again, and pushed into her, wanting to be inside when she completely shattered.

Her legs wound around my hips, hands slid down my back and she pressed her perfect, soft sounds right into my ear, telling me she was close, to move faster, to suck her, harder, and harder.

She was sticky with my orgasm and her milk, with sweat and scotch. Pleasure built brick by brick until it tripped that feeling that was too intense to simply be called pleasure anymore and was nearly painful with how good it was. I kissed her one more time, a gentle growl and the tiny press of teeth before my restraint crumpled and I turned wild, fucking her in a flurry of thrusts, messy and wet.

I ground against her, the tension in me building until it snapped and jerked above, coming with a sharp groan.

Beneath me, Sara let out hoarse, moaning cries that broke with very rhythmic clenching around me.

"Max," she whispered and pulled me close, the movement grating me against her sensitive skin so she shuddered at the friction. I began to pull back but she stopped me with her hands sliding down my sweaty back. "Stay in me."

I caught my breath in the soft space beside her neck, halfheartedly working to keep my weight off her. Her nails scratched lightly up and down my back, legs still curled around my hips.

"All right?"

Beside me, she nodded.

"That was fun," I whispered playfully, and felt her smile when she kissed my cheek.

"Welcome back, Mr. and Mrs. Stella," she said.

∽

WE RODE TOGETHER IN the back of the car, with Scott up front, navigating us through the streets of Manhattan. I felt uncorked, able to release pressure for the first time in months, and it occurred to me only now that I'd been rather terrified: I hadn't known whether Sara and I would ever find our way back directly to each other, or if from now on there would forever be something else—

children, careers, the gradual bricklaying of life itself—bridging us.

I would have been all right if it had gone that way, if the secret we had and shared had faded away and we had to learn to find our intimacy in other ways. But knowing how easily we could go back to that, and anytime, relieved something a bit guilty and dark inside.

"What are you thinking?" she asked, as she always did, right when I wanted to admit my thoughts the least.

"Something rather dickish."

"Ooh, then you *have* to tell me."

I turned to her, took her hand in both of mine. "I was thinking that I'm relieved we still have this. That if it had gone away, I would have been okay, but I think I would have been a bit devastated at first, too. I can share you with any number of kids, as long as there is a piece there that remains only mine."

"There's more than one piece that is only yours," she said, looking mildly surprised. "That's what our marriage is. It's the thing between us that we take care of, knowing that someday it will only be us in that enormous apartment again."

"If you want more kids, you know we can't stay in Manhattan forever," I told her.

She put her fingers over my lips, saying, "Shh. Let's enjoy this new baseline for a bit."

We both straightened, seeming to realize in unison

that we hadn't heard our phones go off the entire time we'd been at the club.

"Shit," she whispered, digging in her purse. "Did I turn it off?"

"I know I didn't," I said, pulling mine from my pocket. It was just that there were no texts, no missed calls, nothing.

I quickly typed a message to Niall: All good? We're headed home.

His reply came almost immediately. Everything is fine. Anna is asleep. See you soon.

NIALL WAS STRETCHED OUT on the leather couch in the living room, watching John Oliver on the telly. Anna was asleep on his long legs, one fist in her mouth and the other curled around her lion blanket.

"Good night out then?" he asked quietly, watching as we hung our coats up in the closet.

"The best," I told him, taking in the scene in front of me. "Are you sure you don't want to move in across the hall? There's a flat for sale. This would be very convenient for us."

He laughed. "It's tempting. Your building is rather posh, and this little one is brilliant, yeah?"

"Cheers, mate," I said quietly. "You let us forget to be worried."

He smiled up at me, giving me that look that told me he thought I was a sentimental wanker, and then rested his hand on Anna's belly. "It was really nice. Perhaps you can return the favor someday." His smile straightened for the span of a heartbeat, and in that tiny flicker in his expression, I felt the full weight of his disappointment in his marriage.

"Without a doubt," I reassured him.

Sara went to change out of her dress and I reached for Anna, picking her up with the confidence of a father who expects the child to remain sleeping. Except she didn't; for once she woke when jostled, and her sweet little face screwed up in frustration as she began to cry.

"Ah, sorry, sorry," I whispered, bouncing her gently. "Just a minute, little miss, your mum's almost done."

Anna didn't want to be held and rocked, she wanted Sara, and the sound of her angry cry pushed an ache into my chest. But it didn't bother me the way it would have only days ago. I felt recharged like a battery, full of patience and calm and the quiet that comes from genuine contentment.

Sara came into the hall, taking the baby from me, and I followed them both into the nursery, watching them settle into the rocking chair.

"You're a lovely sight, my two girls."

"She's probably the cutest baby on the planet," Sara said, grinning up at me. So relaxed, so fucking giddy. It was as if she knew all along we would end up right here, in this night.

   I bent down, kissed Annabel's soft cheek as she calmed down and began to nurse. "You got your sensitive side from your daddy," I whispered. "Sorry about that, baby girl. But you also got your mum's steel, so you'll be okay."